Bello:

hidden talent redisc

Bello is a digital only imprint of Pan Macmillan,
established to breathe new life into previously published,
classic books.

At Bello we believe in the timeless power of the imagination,
of good story, narrative and entertainment and we want to use
digital technology to ensure that many more readers
can enjoy these books into the future.

We publish in ebook and Print on Demand formats
to bring these wonderful books to new audiences.

About Bello:

www.panmacmillan.com/bello

*Sign up to our newsletter to hear about
new releases, events and competitions:*

www.panmacmillan.com/bellonews

Jo Bannister

Jo Bannister lives in Northern Ireland, where she worked as a journalist and editor on local newspapers. Since giving up the day job, her books have been shortlisted for a number of awards. Most of her spare time is spent with her horse and dog, or clambering over archaeological sites. She is currently working on a new series of psychological crime/thrillers.

Jo Bannister

THE MATRIX

BELL

First published in 1981 by Hale

This edition published 2012 by Bello
an imprint of Pan Macmillan, a division of Macmillan Publishers Limited
Pan Macmillan, 20 New Wharf Road, London N1 9RR
Basingstoke and Oxford
Associated companies throughout the world

www.panmacmillan.com/imprints/bello

ISBN 978-1-4472-3648-1 EPUB
ISBN 978-1-4472-3647-4 POD

A CIP catalogue record for this book is available from the British Library.

Printed and bound by CPI Group (UK) Ltd, Croydon, CR0 4YY

Visit **www.panmacmillan.com** to read more about all our books
and to buy them. You will also find features, author interviews and
news of any author events, and you can sign up for e-newsletters
so that you're always first to hear about our new releases.

Chapter One

He moved through the spaceport as unconsciously at ease amid its complexities and confusion as if he owned it. In fact he had never been there before, but spaceports differed little from the hub of the galaxy to its outermost ring and he had seen a lot of them in the last few years. Sometimes it felt as if he had seen nothing else.

His luggage comprised two items: a soft grip that was more an overnight bag than a weekender, and a guitar. The occasional head turned as he passed, the eyes following him with idle curiosity, the brows wrinkled in stillborn recognition. Many or most of the people in the building would have seen him at some time on their videos, but very few could have put a name to his face or even explained their sense of familiarity.

Familiar or not, he was an arresting figure. In one of the oldest segments of the Alliance, peopled mainly by short, broad Slavs, he was tall and slender, his skin had a golden cast and his eyes tilted upwards at their outer corners. His eyes were dark but not black; smoky brown, very calm beneath the slanted lids. Above the widely spaced eyes the forehead was broad and unlined, shaded by a thick fringe of fine dark hair which fell almost as far as his thin, upswept eyebrows. High cheekbones and a narrow jaw gave his face a pointed shape. His lips were thin, but an upward curve suggested that an accident of nature rather than a mean disposition was responsible. You would have said he was Japanese but for his height, and his eyes and some abstract air about him that was not wholly oriental. He was a Eurasian, a child of mixed races, mixed traditions.

Even his clothes set him apart. They were not remarkable in themselves, being black, plain except for a soft rippling shimmer as he moved, and comfortably loose; but they contrasted markedly with the gay, gaudy colours flaring all around him. Like a black swan gliding through a cackle of flamingoes he moved purposefully, alone and self-contained, through the weary, querulous, waiting bands of transit travellers.

They were mostly holidaymakers. Virtually no one was staying here: they were waiting for transfer flights somewhere brighter, somewhere gayer. The young man in black was not on holiday, and had reached his destination. There was no way of knowing what he was doing here, except that he was not a commercial traveller. The only impression he gave was a personal one: of an intelligent, thoughtful, confident young man whose mixed ancestry was no more important to him than the careless stares of his fellow travellers.

The guitar was one clue to what he was and his strange dark eyes, seeing both clearly and deeply, were another. He was a poet, and his name was Dak Hamiko.

He located the information bureau, which was sited where spaceport information bureaux are always sited, and identified himself. "Have you a message for me?"

The girl, in regulation magenta pseudosilk, consulted her console. "No, sir."

Dak frowned, taken aback. "Are you sure?"

The girl looked at him for the first time. "Quite sure." The resentment at having her efficiency questioned, which she managed to keep out of her voice, showed in her eyes.

Dak felt in his pocket for the slip of paper but the mistake was not his. This was the place, he had arrived on the specified flight – he must be expected. He looked from the slip to the girl again and smiled, not apologetically but with something which disposed her to feel more warmly towards him. "Could you check it for me? In case there's been some hold-up somewhere."

She did and the result was as before. "I'm sorry, Mr Hamiko, there really is nothing for you. Who were you expecting? – I could always call them for you."

Dak's smile went impish around the corners. "I'm afraid I don't know."

The girl's warmth, which was not wholly native to her, faded quickly with the suspicion that she was being taken advantage of. "I beg your pardon."

"Absurd, isn't it? I've come from the Twelfth Circle and it's taken me three months, following a trail of anonymous messages I don't even understand, and now I'm here there's no one to meet me. Thank you for your trouble."

He turned away, still smiling, but suddenly he felt inestimably weary. Even his scant luggage bore him down, so that he hefted the guitar on to his back and switched the grip to his other hand. Weeks of spacelag which he had resolutely refused to acknowledge, too many days among crowds, too many nights in transit lounges; all the fatigue which he had been able to control because always when he arrived there was another message drawing him on: all of that caught up with him when the anticipated adrenalin failed to flow. For a moment the bright lights danced; he may actually have swayed. When they cleared he bought a hot drink from a dispenser and found somewhere to sit down.

It had begun in a hotel room on Scapula. He did not remember the name of the hotel, or even of the city. He had been singing in the night-palaces. Returning late one evening he found an envelope containing a teleprinted message and a spaceflight ticket. The message was short and cryptic and made no sense. The ticket was for a one-way trip to Epho, a dusty staging-post for the older vessels which could not make the starjumps, leaving the next morning.

He did not know now why he had taken it. He knew no one on Epho. The message was not an offer of work; not an offer of any kind. There was no money in the envelope – indeed, he might have found it easier to ignore if there had been. But the enigma of an incomprehensible message and the uncompromising challenge of a space ticket in his name proved irresistible.

His imagination, sparked in a seedy hotel room on strobe-and-plastic Scapula, remained afire with curiosity throughout the five-day hop to Epho. He envisaged all manner of ends to his strange odyssey. Reality was a bitter disappointment. All that awaited him was another envelope, another message, another ticket pushing him on to Tyxl in the Tenth Circle. After that the journeys became longer. It made sense psychologically. No man could be expected to commit himself to a three-month journey at the whim of a total stranger; but the right man might hazard five days on the chance of an interesting experience. Five days from home he might be prepared to travel another week rather than return unsatisfied; and after that a fortnight; and after that whatever was demanded of him. So Dak travelled between envelopes through the uncaring infinity of space.

There had been eight of them. Eight strips of teleprinter tape, eight space tickets. Eight nights spent curled on flabby spaceport couches, his head pillowed on his bag, waiting for early morning flights to places he had hardly heard of and Zen knew where beyond. Eight stewardesses welcoming him aboard, eight life-and-souls-of-the-party petitioning him for entertainment on the long flights and not understanding his songs; eight sets of male passengers mystified by his disinterest in gambling and eight sets of female passengers resenting his polite disinterest in them. Young men travelling the space lanes alone were traditionally after one or the other, often both.

And now it had ended: here on Ganymede, in the dead old heart of the Alliance, in a spaceport he could not have distinguished from a dozen others except that this one held no waiting message. As the hot, tasteless liquid from the plastic cup revived him, Dak began to grow angry at the unseen decoyman who had lured him so far, at such cost to his time and energy, only to abandon him parsecs from anywhere, on a grotty little moon circling an exhausted planet circling a diminishing sun of only historic importance. Had it been no more than an expensive prank, a rich man's practical joke? Was someone sitting out there somewhere behind a spy-viewer, giggling helplessly as he stumbled from solar system to solar system at the random bidding of a teleprinter? And for why? Because he had fancied a note of yearning in that first meaningless message,

4

and because he had once promised on his honour as a poet to take everything life threw at him.

So here he was, on Ganymede, with no message, no money, no friends, nowhere to go, nothing to do and no strength left with which to do it. Lost, lonely, mentally and physically exhausted, Dak Hamiko wanted nothing so much as to crawl into a dark hole and hibernate. With his head resting on his arms on the table and his dark hair spilling on to its plastic surface, he lapsed into sleep.

He woke to the sound of his name, unsubtly distorted by the public address system, to a rawness as of carbolic in his eyes and a taste like a tannery in his mouth. Groping for awareness he knocked the plastic cup to the floor. It bounced once and rolled away. He gathered his senses loosely about him and, leaving his belongings, went to the information desk.

It was a different girl in the same near-fluorescent magenta. "Mr Hamiko? Phone call for you."

Dak stiffened, instantly alert, nerves tense. Under the tangled hair his eyes brightened with hope. He made a conscious effort to relax the muscles that were clamping his chest and followed the girl's gesture to a booth.

There was a video-screen but the caller had chosen not to use it. In the blank grey glass Dak could see a faint reflection of himself and behind him the desultory movement of people who wished they were in bed. He said, "I am Dak Hamiko."

"You have come a long way, Dak Hamiko." The voice sounded remote: possibly because of great distance, but more like over a great gulf. It was cold, mechanical. The words could have been a welcome. The tone could not.

Striving against disappointment, Dak said simply, "I got your message."

"And understood it?" For a moment the cool voice seemed to kindle. Dak wished there was a face to go with it.

"Not really."

"Then why did you come?"

"Space travel is expensive. I assumed it was important."

"It is. You should have understood the message. It was specifically

5

designed to be read by a person of your intellect and experience."

"Then perhaps you overestimated me." The least edge was creeping into Dak's voice. He had imagined this ultimate encounter a hundred times. Not once had it gone anything like this.

"You were the optimum choice. That is not to say the perfect choice."

"Perfection is a concept which exists only inside the brain of a computer."

Again Dak sensed rather than heard a quickening of interest. "Why do you say that?"

"Because it's true. I should know. All poets seek perfection, and at the same time know they are as incapable of attaining it, of even approaching it with their outstretched fingers, as a spastic is of dancing *Swan Lake*; as a nettle is of breeding with a rose."

"You are the one. I was right." It might have been Dak's imagination, or it could have been a fractional satisfaction in the distant voice. Dak felt a sudden inexplicable chill.

"What one? What do you want with me? Why have you brought me here?"

"You are where you are of your own free will. Remain, or return, or continue, as you choose."

"Continue to where?" Dak was vaguely aware that his voice was unsteady. "Where are you? Who are you? What do you want with me?"

"No passenger ships travel deeper into this system than Ganymede," stated the other, obliquely. "But the day after tomorrow a helium miner will call *en route* to Sol. Be on board when it leaves. Have them land you on Terra." The connection broke abruptly, finally, leaving Dak staring at the blank screen, mentally if not actually open-mouthed.

It was the most ludicrous thing he had heard in his life. Terra? Terra was a desert, a burnt-up dustbowl. Centuries of over-population and over-exploitation had reduced it to a sterile cinder. Some people, the rich and the clever, had got away in time, joined their second cousins on the colonised worlds of the Alliance. Those who remained ended their days all together, in an ultimate holocaust.

He did not know if there was a spaceport, even a staging depot. He had never heard of people going there. He could not ask a crew of hard-headed helium miners to take him there for the pittance that was all he could offer. They'd kick his head in.

Ganymede itself was not exactly the hub of the space-lanes. The next flight anywhere he cared to go was three days hence: three days in which to make the money to ride it. Enough, on the pleasure planets circling Deneb or in the cultural cities of the Antares cluster. But on dull and dusty Ganymede, the last remaining outpost of a degenerate system, the locus of transients, ageing spacecrew on the beach and those who preyed on either – how would a poet fare here? He booked into the cheapest room he could find, sat down on the bed to think about it, and fell asleep in his clothes.

He spent forty-eight hours in limbo. Nobody was interested in his songs or in him. For the first time in his life he went hungry, conserving his slender resources against a passage off Ganymede, back to some world he knew. He could find no work, not as a poet or anything else. On Ganymede what was not done by computers was done by robots: there was no casual labour for a man. He understood why the bars here were filled with washed-up old greasers off the starships: paid off as past their usefulness, they drank or gambled away their severance pay and could never afterward make enough money to leave. Dak was young, healthy, master of a certain talent, but still seemed unable to earn his ticket out. All he had worth selling was his guitar. He would as soon have sold his right arm.

He walked. Away from the spaceport, beyond the shops and bars, until the street became a lane and then a track, running through nothing but the dust of former fields. There was nothing out here but the occasional untidy cluster of derelict prefab sheds, but away from the perennial glare of the neon city a man could look up and see the stars. Dak Hamiko never tired of looking at the stars. He supposed it was because he was a poet. Or else why.

As he watched, the stars began to pale, as though with impending dawn. But Sol was a long way away, so that even full in the sky the best she gave to Ganymede was a kind of nacrous twilight, and now that pearly zone was on the far side of the little moon. The glowering rim which rose above the horizon was ochre, leprous and vast: malignant Jupiter, whose light fell so ominously on civilised eyes that the incomers of the Alliance preferred to make their own, as they made their own atmosphere.

Back at the rooming-house he found two men waiting for him. One wore the uniform of the Security Corps: it was the same all over the Twelve Circles, only the insignia on the buttons varied. The other showed an egophotic plaque identifying him as an officer of the same body. They approached as Dak came in off the street, at a nod from the proprietor, who disappeared immediately into a back office.

"Hamiko?"

"I am Dak Hamiko."

"You're to come with us. To Security Centre. We have some questions for you."

"In what connection?"

The officer scowled. The other man hefted the weapon that was part of his uniform as if hoping for a chance to use it. "Don't get clever with us, sonny. You know your rights. You should know ours too. You refuse to help us in our enquiries, we're entitled to blast you all over the ceiling."

"Only if I offer to use arms or violence to resist arrest," Dak countered calmly. He was not versed in customary law, but he had travelled enough and read enough to know that nowhere in the Alliance – not even on benighted Ganymede – had state servants the power of autonomous murder.

The man's scowl deepened. "Are you resisting?"

"Are you arresting me?"

"Yes."

"Then no." He went quickly, without further protest either verbal or physical. There was no need for them to manacle his wrists behind his back and manhandle him out to their vehicle like a dangerous felon. He submitted with as much tranquil dignity as he could muster, in the hope of making them feel silly, but the tactic was lost on them. In the flivver he asked what he was accused of. The uniformed man, who was driving, told him to shut up and the other said he'd find out soon enough. Dak suspected they didn't know.

At Security Centre they stripped him, searching for contraband. After his clothes had been examined they were returned, silently, and he was locked in a dark cell. He was not told why or for how long. A practising pacifist since adolescence, Dak knew precisely how to turn their physical victory over him into a psychological defeat. He lay on the cold floor, began to regulate his breathing, deliberately relaxed every muscle in his body – working from his toes upwards – until he slipped painlessly into a sleep-trance. So far as an observer could know he had blithely fallen asleep; but the cortex, the new logical part of his brain, remained conscious and functioning. The inducement of sleep-trance was the most effective way he knew of gaining a breathing-space for meditation free from interference.

Whatever offence the Security Corps had arrested him for he was innocent. He had committed no crime, either here recently or anywhere else at any time. He knew no one who led so indecently blameless a life as he. So his arrest was a mistake or a put-up job. In the latter case, and also possibly in the former, someone had gone out of his way to make Dak's life difficult. Because people did not involve the Security Corps in small matters of disagreement and dislike, he had to assume it was someone with a serious grudge against him. He did not remember offending anyone that much. Unless the anonymous voice on the phone, the enigmatic composer of obscure messages, had some way of knowing that he did not intend to go to Terra. The thought was alarming, because the decision existed only in his own mind. But it was also compelling, because he knew no one on Ganymede, no one else knew of his presence here, and no one else had reason to care whether he was here or not.

He was aroused from his trance by a boot in the ribs – not a kick, really, more a poke – and strong lights. After the darkness in the cell the light made him blink, and blinking made him feel defensive. He made an effort to control the reaction until his eyes adjusted to the glare. Not for the first time he blessed the tiny, gentle woman who had taught him that his body was his to command.

Barefoot, swinging his sandals by their straps, he allowed himself to be marched down a corridor to an office and stood before the broad desk like an errant schoolboy. The man behind the desk did not look up.

"I am Dak Hamiko."

He might not have spoken. The man showed no sign of having heard; only the dark furrows between his heavy brows deepened a fraction more. His brow, bent over papers on his desk, and the top of his head were all Dak could see of him.

Dak allowed his sandals to drop on the desk. In the pregnant silence of the room the sound was shocking. The man behind the desk started as if shot at and glared furiously from Dak to his escort. The man raised his weapon, then lowered it. You could not shoot a man for dropping his sandals any more than you could for asking questions, even on Ganymede.

"I know who you are." The reply was belated and given with a bad grace.

"I don't know who you are."

"I am –" He paused, frowning harder, caught between the indignity of having to introduce himself and the childishness of refusing to. "Captain Vorachenko."

"So tell me what I can do for you," invited Dak. His face remained inscrutable, but in the secret depths of his mind he was chuckling. There is no better way of annoying a bully than by offering to do as a favour what he wants to make you do by force. He didn't think he was in any real danger and it amused him to bait these humourless petty autocrats.

Captain Vorachenko was building up a visible head of steam. "You are Dak Hamiko, of Tok-ai-Do in the Sixth Circle, and I have instructions to deport you aboard the first craft leaving Ganymede. I shall endeavour to ensure that you have an uncomfortable journey."

"Why?"

The word posed two questions. Vorachenko, unable to answer the second, chose to understand by it the first. "Because you're an undesirable alien and if we didn't deport your sort Ganymede would become the rubbish dump of the Galaxy. There's a ship leaving the spaceport in an hour's time. I don't care where you go so long as you don't come back here."

Dak said, "Who says I'm undesirable?"

Vorachenko stared at him, momentarily nonplussed. "Our computer, naturally. Do you suppose we're provincial dwarfs out here, having no contact with the Alliance? We've got communications, you know, we've got computers. We know what you've been up to out there."

"What?"

"Enough to qualify you as an undesirable alien, you disgusting little pervert," snapped Vorachenko. "I doubt if you'll ever make planetfall again: every time you land there'll be someone waiting with a copy of your criminal record ready to shove you back into space. You might get down on Epho. I can't promise, but they're pretty easy there. They can afford to be, they've virtually no one left still capable of being corrupted."

"I've been to Epho," volunteered Dak. "But I haven't got a criminal record."

Captain Vorachenko looked at him. Looked at the sheet of paper uppermost before him. Shook his head disbelievingly. "Get him out of here. Get him out of my sight. Get him on that ship and off this moon, and, by God, Hamiko, if you set a foot in my province again I'll chop it off at the ankle!"

Totally bewildered, Dak suffered his escort to drag him backwards from the office while he wondered dizzily if his sojourn on Ganymede could have had any more satisfactory conclusion than a free passage away after two days. He had only one grief. Hooking his heel around the doorpost to halt his progress he said, "What about my guitar?"

"Your belongings will be waiting at the spaceport. Go!" Dak's sandals flew across the room and hit him in the chest, and the door slammed shut.

Dak celebrated his good fortune in silence all the way to the spaceport. He received his papers with a cheerful unregret which infuriated his guard. His first misgivings came with a view from the terminal building across the concrete desert outside to a vessel which was no passenger ship and unlike any cargo tramp he had ever seen.

It was not that it lacked size. It was bigger than all save the greatest of inter-stellar liners, but its shape was utterly alien. Most of its vast bulk was given over to tanks of some kind. The flight-deck was at the stern, over the engines: at the front was a colossal maw like nothing so much as a giant vacuum-cleaner. The streamlined star-drive was conspicuous by its absence. The whole great vessel was massively heatshielded, but charred black where the flames of a hundred suns had licked at its skin. Hunched in surpassing ugliness on its concrete pad, dwarfing the short-haul ferries which were the only other vessels on the apron that morning, it might have been a great brooding beetle.

Dak had never seen anything like it. All the same, he could have made a shrewd guess at what it was.

A shove from behind propelled him towards the exit. He lurched and staggered, off balance, and was halfway down the ramp before he got a proper look at the man who had pushed him. It was not often Dak had to look up at someone. He decided, on the whole, not to protest. "Do you know about my gear –?"

"On board. Hurry up. You've held us up enough already."

"It wasn't my idea."

The man looked at him and something like a smile twisted his dark features. "No, I don't suppose it was. What did you do?"

"Nothing."

The man looked frankly unconvinced. He also looked as if he habitually tore the arms of liars. "They're not deporting you for something to do. It costs them money to get you a passage even on a helium miner."

"I dropped my sandals on the captain's desk," Dak offered lamely.

The man laughed and shook his head, and pushed Dak ahead

of him down the ramp; more gently than before, but Dak was still running when he reached the bottom. There he stopped, turned and waved goodbye – to his escort, who pretended not to notice, to the spaceport, to Ganymede, and to his two days of rebellion.

The big man was Sharm, first mate of the *Leviathan*. The captain was a shorter individual, nearly as broad as he was tall, called Divik, who was also the majority shareholder in the vessel and her load. *Leviathan* was owned, as many of the older craft were, by the crew in direct proportion to their status aboard. Once in space *Leviathan* was a mobile autonomous state and Divik was master under God.

Dak feared Divik on sight. His squat body was as tough and hard from the hard life as Sharm's massive frame, but where Sharm's expression was occasionally lightened by a flicker of humour the overwhelming impulse behind Divik's was always and only greed. Since Dak had taken his talent and his guitar and left home he had known discomfort, loneliness, depression, but never fear. He was surprised to find himself so intimidated by another human being, and attempted to rationalise the feeling. Divik was undoubtedly a malevolent presence but he had no reason to wish Dak any particular harm. But all Dak's instincts warned him off, like nerves shrieking before they are cut. Ashamed of the panic the man engendered in him, he struggled to keep his feelings private.

Divik made no attempt to disguise his feelings about Dak. He carried no passengers, he said. Everybody aboard *Leviathan* worked. If Dak would not work he would be put out with the garbage. Dak believed him, but the overt threat did not worry him as much as the quiet malice lurking in Divik's eyes.

For a week Dak fetched and carried and pulled his weight as well as any unskilled tyro could aboard something as complex and technical as a helium miner heading for helium. After the first couple of days, in which he bore their sporting patiently, he got on well enough with the crew, learning what he could and entertaining them when he had time. Sharm, with his rocklike face and saturnine humour, he positively liked. He would join the mate for the long midnight watch and, uninterrupted for hours at a time, they would trade travellers' tales and Sharm would speak of the battles he had been in, starlight sparkling in his coal-black eyes.

Divik he avoided as much as possible. Usually when he failed to take evasive action Divik found something to berate him for. Often he used his fists – casual blows, not incapacitating; Dak could have tolerated the discomfort philosophically but felt diminished by the careless brutality, which was such as a man might use against an animal, not another man. Once he lost his balance and fell during anti-meteor manoeuvres, and Divik kicked him twice in the ribs before stumping away laughing. The place hurt for days. This went on until Sharm happened to see Dak without his shirt. He said nothing then, but afterwards Divik only sneered a lot while the hatred in his eyes grew.

As *Leviathan* journeyed in towards Sol, Dak was watching the charts. Sharm had shown him how to plot a course four-dimensionally, so as to arrive not only at a given spot but at a time when the spot was occupied, and he knew Terra would be on the right side of its orbit when they passed, and that for a minor detour they could land him there. Still he quailed from approaching Divik with his request.

He sounded Sharm out first. Sharm looked at him as he had the first day. "Terra? You can't be serious. It's a desert – you couldn't live there even if Divik put you down, which he won't. Why by all the stars do you want to go to Terra?"

"I don't. But somebody wants me there and I can't seem to get away from him. He arranged for me to be arrested and put on this ship so that I could get there."

"Who?"

"I don't know."

"Then why?"

"I don't know that either."

"Forget Terra," said Sharm. "Come with us to Sol. You'll get your share of the profits. There are worse things than a helium miner, and one of them is the surface of Terra."

"What's it like?"

Sharm's eyes slipped out of focus and went distant and opaque.

"Terra? Most of the time you can't see it at all, just a big swirl of cloud racing round and never stopping. There's white ice at the poles, and once in a while the clouds break and then the oceans are bright blue. But the land is a dustbowl: mountains and deserts and erosion, and always the sandstorms blasting on, thousands of miles long. You couldn't live in that, Dak. If it didn't strip the flesh from your bones the minute you stepped outside, you'd starve as soon as your rations ran out. Nothing lives down there. Nothing could."

"Yet he wants me there – desperately, it seems. Why, if I couldn't survive? Is it all like that?"

Sharm shrugged. It was like a mountain shrugging. "Who knows? Nobody's looked for a very long time. I'm only telling you what I've seen passing by. I've seen some barren worlds, but none more than that one. The only successful Terrans now are going to be fishes."

"We evolved there, Sharm."

"A very long time ago. Before the desert, before the sandstorms. There are no Earthmen any more."

"All the same," said Dak, standing up, "I'm going to see Divik."

He woke up three hours later, lying on an unfamiliar bunk with a damp cloth across one eye. Sharm was a still, silent bulk in a corner of the cabin, watching him soberly from the shadows. He had been standing there motionless for two hours, since he had finished working on the young man's face. As first mate on a deep-space vessel for many years he had acquired considerable medical expertise. He required all of it, and a very steady hand, to remove the glass shards from Dak's eye without lacerating the cornea irreparably.

He had answered a call to Divik's cabin and found the captain standing over the long, terribly still form, half a crystal Sandaar unit tight clenched in his fist. He was not laughing. He thought he had killed the boy. Sharm lifted Dak wordlessly in his arms and carried him to his own cabin. At first, scrutinising the mess of ravaged flesh and gore, Sharm could not be sure whether the bloody socket still contained an eye. He spent the better part of an hour irrigating, disinfecting, drawing the tatters of skin together in a complex jigsaw. Dak would wear a network of tiny scars around that eye for the rest of his life. But his sight would be unimpaired.

When the pattern of his breathing changed and his good eye finally glinted open ill the gentle half-light, Sharm said roughly, "Keep still unless you want your eyeball to go rolling across the deck."

Memory returned slowly. Dak tried to smile but found that his face was not functioning properly. "I guess he said no."

Sharm did not reply. "Stay where you are. Don't move about and don't touch your face. I shan't be long." He moved towards the hatch.

"Where are you going?"

The big miner paused, considering. "I'm going to thump Divik."

Dak laughed – a weak, unsteady sound born as much of lightheadedness as of humour. "That's not necessary. I'll be all right."

Sharm nodded. "I know you will. That's why I'm going to thump him. If you hadn't woken up I was going to kill him."

"Compromise, and thump him later," suggested Dak. "Tell me where we are."

Sharm, frowning, consulted a monitor on his wall. "Just passing through the orbit of Mars."

Dak had jacked himself up on his elbows to see. "And Terra's the next one in?" Sharm nodded. "Something will happen," Dak said with conviction.

"That's what you told Divik, and why he hit you with the spare Sandaar in spite of the fact that the one in the shaft at the moment is five months old and we can't mine without it. What sort of something?"

"I don't know. I'm only sure that whoever brought me here won't let me get away now. He'll – intervene – in some way if I'm not put down on that planet."

"I've told you, you couldn't live down there. And where would we put you down? There's no spacefield and the damn thing's thirty thousand miles round. Do you know where to go?" Dak shook his head, very slightly. "What continent? What hemisphere, even? It's crazy. Forget about it, come with us."

"It is crazy," Dak agreed, "and I'd willingly forget about it, but I don't think he will. Look. Why do you think I'm here at all? It wasn't my doing, it was his. He had me picked up by the police on Ganymede and deported on to probably the only ship in the galaxy actually travelling towards Terra. I don't know how he did that, but he did. I don't know what he'll do next, but I'll take any odds you're offering that he somehow persuades, coerces or compels Divik to put me down."

After what seemed a long pause Sharm asked, "Are you afraid?"

"I don't think he means me any harm."

"That wasn't the question."

"No. I'm – confused. Apprehensive. I wish I knew what it was all about, what to expect. But no, I don't think I'm afraid." He grinned. "Not the way I am of Divik, anyway."

"Because – well, this is a pretty tough ship. People have tried to take cargos from us before. We haven't lost one yet. If you don't want to go, we can give him a hard time taking you –" Sharm's voice, which had grown low and hesitant with embarrassment, now tailed off altogether.

Dak smiled. "I'm grateful for the offer. But Sharm, I've come a long way for this meeting, mostly of my own free will. If I get scared and run now, I'll spend the rest of my life wondering what it was about."

"Down there the rest of your life may be negligible."

"Somebody wants me there badly enough to bring me from the Twelfth Circle. That's a long way and it's taken a long time. It had to be important. I'm a poet, right? – my job is turning emotions into words. I may not understand the messages I got but I felt the urgency, like an electric current. Like a magnet."

"Like a flame to a moth. You're going to your death."

"I don't believe so."

Neither saw any point in continuing the argument. Sharm knew Divik would brook no interference with his schedule, and knew what *Leviathan*'s armaments were capable of. Dak knew what he was capable of, the other. He thought it possible that the coercion when it came would be psychological rather than tangible. He had persuaded the Security Corps on Ganymede to carry out his plan without giving them any idea that they were being manipulated. If Divik should get a sudden overwhelming urge to see Terra for himself, or alternatively to rid his ship of its Jonah by marooning him on the nearest desert planet, Dak would not have been in the least surprised,

Sharm took the long night watch as *Leviathan* homed in towards the ageing star and, before that, a rendezvous with the orbit of Terra. No one came to bother him or disturb his thoughts. Once he checked on Dak and found him sleeping restlessly, whimpering with pain, actual or remembered, fretful with dreams. Sharm bathed his face without waking him and stayed with him until he slipped into quieter sleep. He went off duty as the ship began its day.

Dak awoke refreshed from his long sleep, feeling in fact better than he had any right to. He washed gingerly, carefully avoiding the bandage someone – presumably Sharm – had replaced during the night. He smiled at the thought of Sharm, the mountain man of deep space, appointing himself nursemaid to a wandering poet.

He found the flight-deck in a state of unformed but barely suppressed tension, and himself the focus of it. Divik eyed him with hatred, the others with mistrust. It wasn't rational, they could not have said what they were afraid of – certainly none of them would have admitted to being afraid of Dak. Yet they felt themselves instinctively, as he did intuitively, to be in the grip of forces they did not understand, and while he associated the sensation with a toneless voice and a blank video-screen they associated it with him. As he passed between them they shot him sidelong glances and shifted away. Sharm was not among them.

He had wondered whether to make any reference to the previous day's events. Now it seemed he had no choice. Hands in pockets, with unconscious grace, he leaned one shoulder against a stanchion and said, "I'm sorry to have caused you concern. This situation is not of my making: I am as much a victim of it as you feel yourselves to be. What I said to Divik was not intended as a threat. Still, I believe you will be obliged to do as I ask. I think it would save a lot of trouble if you'd agree to land me on Terra. It's hardly out of your way: the time it would take surely isn't worth the worry."

Dak thought he had got to know the crew quite well. He thought of several of them as friends of a kind. Now they looked at him with the blank, guarded eyes of strangers. They saw him as something more than a stranger: an alien. Dak felt more conscious of his slanting eyes, of his yellow skin, than at any time since leaving home. He was sorry, because he thought their mistrust could bring them grief. He did not know it would also bring him grief.

He felt the circle around him tighten and moved fractionally to put the stanchion at his back. With a calm that was more apparent than actual he scanned the tense faces, searching for the one less hostile one that he could use as a key to the others. He found no chink in the armoured wall around him.

"Trust me," he said. "I mean you no harm."

Divik had moved through the circle and stood now before Dak like an accuser. Dak looked down at him and finally understood why of all of them Divik, short and without greatness, was master of *Leviathan*. Whatever the rest of them felt, Divik was unafraid, even of the unknown. Savagely intolerant of any challenge to his command, his sovereignty or his profit, an unreasonable and implacable enemy, he was none the less twice as much a man as any member of his crew except Sharm. Oddly, Dak's prime reaction was a clearer, kinder understanding of his own fear of the man.

"Who are you?" Divik's voice was low with venom. "What are you? What are you doing on my ship?"

"I am what I told you. Nothing more. My name is Dak Hamiko, of Tok-ai-Do in the Sixth Circle, and I am a poet. I am on your ship because the police on Ganymede thought I was something else. They were mistaken."

"You're a spy. Have you got friends out here, waiting to board us?"

"You have nothing worth stealing."

Divik paused momentarily, frowning, remembering that the tanks were empty. "The ship herself, then."

"Privateers take passenger ships, not miners. They're not interested in working for a living."

Divik did not answer. His eyes strayed away from Dak's face, and when they returned his dark features had gone hard and blank. The atypical softness in his voice only confirmed the suspicion in the pit of Dak's stomach that Divik had reached a decision, and it was nothing for Dak to celebrate. He wished desperately that Sharm was here, but was too proud to call out his name.

A knife had appeared in Divik's hand. He stood very close to Dak and touched its point to his throat. Dak felt it plucking at the skin and the sudden sensation that was more warmth than pain when the skin parted and the blood began to flow. "I think perhaps, for safety's sake," said Divik, "I should kill you now."

Dak's tone was still calm, but all his self-control was not enough to keep the hoarseness from his voice. "It would be safer still to do as I ask."

"You think your friends will avenge you? They need a saboteur on board to take this ship – that's why you're here. They'll keep clear of us after we throw them your carcass."

"You're wrong about me."

Divik smiled. Dak had not seen him smile before. It was an experience he could have borne to miss. "Nowhere near as wrong as you were about us."

He barked orders. The miners fell on Dak as if he were a dangerous animal, pinning his limbs, rendering him helpless. Surging panic made him want to struggle but he resisted, knowing struggle to be pointless and detrimental to whatever clear thinking he might yet be capable of.

One of them lashed his wrists tightly before him. Another slung a length of cable over an overhead beam. He thought they were going to hang him, but they looped the line between his hands and drew it tight until he hung suspended, his toes brushing the deck. The pain in his wrists was severe. He hardly noticed it.

Cool air washed against his skin as Divik tore the shirt from his back. Then he swung him round and, grinning, shook a metal rod in his face. "It's a tension screw. It's actually a long, thin spring."

Probably unconsciously, Divik was licking his lips. "Very thin, very flexible. It'll rip the hide from your back like barbed wire. You're thin, kid, we'll be down to bare bone in no time. I give you two minutes at the most, and then you'll tell me everything you know."

"I've already told you everything I know."

Divik spun him back against the stanchion. The metal was cold against his hot cheek. He had never known real pain. Neither his parents nor anyone he had encountered on Tok-ai-Do had believed in physical punishment. It had made it easy to be a pacifist. He wondered bleakly how long his command, his oriental inscrutability, would last with Divik tearing his skin from him in strips.

The first cut was so shocking, so surprising in its profound effect on his flesh, that he was not tempted to cry out. As well protest a volcano or a bolt of lightning. The rod seared him from shoulder to waist, like a fine-honed blade of fire, sending duller petals of flame licking up into his head and down his legs. His good eye flew wide and his clenched teeth parted with amazement that anything could hurt so much. His stunned mind reeled between wishing it could give Divik something to make him stop and relief that nothing vital hung on his endurance. He did not know how much of this he could have taken for the worthiest principle in the universe.

Shock gave him no protection from subsequent blows. He felt the resilient coil slice through his skin and thunder against his bones – shoulder, spine and ribs. Repetition made the blows echo in his brain while his whole body responded with a dull ache. The pain across his back was white, the resonance in his head scarlet, the ache in his limbs maroon. Sweat broke out all over him, mingling on his face with tears squeezed from his tight-shut eye, on his back with the blood beginning to trickle from diagonal lacerations two feet long. Blood thundered in his ears and his breath came in gasps. After the first time he wasn't sure if he cried out or not.

A whirlwind exploded onto the flight-deck, scattering the crew like leaves, sending Divik sprawling into one corner, the metal rod clattering into another. Sharm's monstrous anger filled the room, so that a dozen strong men drew back. With one slash of his hand he clove the taut cable, catching Dak as he fell, thrusting his knife into Dak's bound hands. Then he turned back to deal with Divik.

If, bursting on to the flight-deck in response to a clamour as of a hunting-pack, Sharm had let Dak hang the extra moment it would have taken him to rip out Divik's throat, which was what he intended to do now, in all likelihood that would have been the end of it. But Sharm himself had taken such a beating once, as a young man many years before, and long after the scars subsided and time had softened the memory of pain the humiliation remained. So he left Divik alive long enough to cut Dak down, and now Divik had his own knife out. Weapons had sprouted from the hands of his crewmen too, including laser pistols whose effects on the insides of the spaceship would be at least as dreadful as on the human body.

Himself unarmed, Sharm backed up slowly. Powerful hands extended before him in a pose of self-defence, he looked as dangerous as any three of his former friends and colleagues.

Dak had given up trying to free his wrists with Sharm's knife and had turned it outward upon the crew, holding it determinedly in both hands, crouching instinctively although the strain stretched his wounds cruelly wide. When they were back to back Sharm stopped, waiting for Divik to launch his attack. He said, "Sorry, kid." Dak did not reply, for fear that his voice would crack on his pain. In a last, absurd gesture of defiance he tore the bandage from his damaged eye in the hope of seeing that little sooner, that little clearer, the advent of his death.

It didn't happen. Over the husky sibilance of irregular male breathing came the flat, clear monotone of a reporting system. "Unidentified craft approaching on the port flank. Three hundred miles and closing."

Fear and anticipation in the room pulsed like a giant heart lurching. Nobody spoke, or moved, or breathed, for a space of seconds. Then Divik was diving for the command console, searching the visualiser for the first positive trace, ordering his men to *Leviathan*'s guns. Slowly, suspiciously, surrounded by a guard suddenly shrunk to half its size and with its attention diverted elsewhere, Sharm and Dak Hamiko straightened up in the centre of the room. After a moment, uncertainly, Dak offered Sharm the knife and Sharm freed his hands.

Despite the fact that Divik had not opened a communications channel a voice bludgeoned into the room through the radio grid. The words as much as the imperious monotone struck Dak with forceful familiarity.

"You have arrived, Dak Hamiko. Prepare to embark on the lander which is approaching you."

Dak found Sharm staring at him as if he had not heard, or not believed, anything he had said since leaving Ganymede. Weak and dizzy with trauma, he looked around him, took a few steps towards the console and then stumbled. Sharm reached for him but other hands caught him first.

"Bring him over here." With a sweep of his hand up a bank of switches Divik opened a broad band of channels and spoke into the microphone. "All right, you out there, listen to me. You pull back or you get this one without the benefit of a suit. Come after this ship and we'll blast you to kingdom come. We've no cargo and a hell of a lot of guns."

There was a fractional, assimilatory pause. The voice when it spoke again was a tone lower and sounded guarded. "I do not want your ship or your cargo. I have no use for them. I require Dak Hamiko to be put aboard the lander which is closing with your craft. When he is safely aboard you will be allowed to proceed without further hindrance."

"You're not hearing me," sneered Divik. "Hamiko stays with me. You try to interfere with us, I'll carve him up – here, so you can hear him."

Again the tone of voice altered slightly, though there was no knowing what it meant. "Dak Hamiko, are you hurt?"

Dak saw no point in lying. "Yes."

"Nothing to how he's going to be if you don't butt out of here."

The impossible happened. *Leviathan*, which had been travelling at thousands of miles an hour, stopped dead. All her impulsion vanished, dissipated in a split second, absorbed by some incalculable power. Incredibly she did not pull herself apart with the left-over velocity; yet more remarkably, the men inside her were neither crushed nor dismembered by the colossal forces invoked. They felt nothing other than a jerk and the curious sensation of hanging immobile in space. It was as if the vessel's momentum had been instantly and painlessly converted into entropy.

Sharm moved. Taking advantage of the total disorientation of the crew he hurled himself at Divik, grabbing a laser, grabbing Dak. Divik screamed with fury; others shouted – whether with fear or excitement it was impossible to tell; lasers flared with a chilling disregard for *Leviathan*'s life-support systems; and the primary warning siren shrieked its awful message, that the flight-deck was depressurising.

Dak felt Sharm's forearm lock like a band of iron across his chest; heard the shouting, saw the wash of light from the lasers; heard the siren begin its banshee wail of coming death. Then Sharm pulled him hard against his own body, covering them with his weapon. Dak felt the metal studs of Sharm's clothing grind into his ravaged back, saw the lights begin to twinkle and then to bloom, heard a concentrate of every sound on the flight-deck pounding inside his head, and knew nothing more.

Chapter Two

He dreamed. He dreamed that he was dead and a great white worm came to feed on him. He was lying on his side with a strange oblique view of the flight-deck when the hatch opened to admit the sinuous white monster. It was very long, for its far end never came through the door. Making a faint clattering vaguely reminiscent of a dishwasher it nosed its way towards him. Its nose had a pincer grip at the end. He supposed it was all right. If he was dead he couldn't feel anything, and the degree of detachment with which he viewed its progress suggested that all was proceeding as it should; and, anyway, there was no point in bucking the system. Earth to earth, ashes to ashes, dust to dust, and Dak Hamiko to a great space worm.

When it reached him the worm lifted its head and, though blind, appeared to eye him quizzically. It looked him up and down and then leaned over him and looked from the other side. Then it rolled him carefully on to his face. Its touch was gentle and cool against his bare skin. It struck him as odd that, though dead, he could still distinguish between warmth and cold. Considering that gave him a sickening suspicion of wrongness, and when the creature softly drew its questing nose across the crusting wounds in his back the return of the vivid pain filled him with indescribable horror and turned the worm, whose appearance had seemed natural and inevitable, into an object of terror. He fought the worm, thrashing and screaming, but gently and unhurriedly it wrapped its sinuous yielding body around his limbs and held him in the tender, total grip of an alien lover. At the last, before the creature drew him back into the darkness beyond the airlock, desperately he reached out his one free hand towards Sharm, stretching until every cut on his back broke open; but Sharm was also dead and made no move to help him. The worm lifted him carefully over the hatchway and the airlock closed, shutting out the light.

Returning to the Matrix, the servitor placed the limp and bloody form face down on a bed. It cut the ragged clothes from him, cleaned and dressed his wounds and covered him with a sheet before withdrawing. After three months and light-years they had come together, the unconscious young man and the unsleeping Matrix.

While Dak remained unconscious the servitor nursed him with skill and every appearance of concern, and the Matrix watched. Watched while the open wounds knit to silver threads across the golden skin; watched while the fever-chills that shook him subsided and senselessness passed into sleep; watched him grow calm and languid as sleep healed both his body and his mind. When the electrodes which the servitor had attached to Dak's temples and wrists indicated a return to awareness, the Matrix said, "Welcome to Earth, Dak Hamiko."

Dak, rising slowly through the levels of consciousness, heard the words without taking them in. He was rediscovering himself in a new dimension where pain was gone, where fear was a buried memory and the causes for it forgotten, where he was comfortable and safe and strong enough to face the world again. The first thing he was consciously aware of was white light, not bright but soft, reflective, in his face. The whiteness, and something about the soft, shiny smooth surface beneath his chest and against his cheek, reminded him momentarily of the worm, but he couldn't see the connection and his senses, still vague and half coherent, left the worm and drifted on to explore other stimulae.

The air he breathed tasted clean – very clean. Without realising it he had grown accustomed to the chemically adequate but weary, uninspiring fug churned out by the recycling systems of spaceships and artificial atmosphere plants. The stuff breezing through his head and lungs now was like champagne compared not with ale but with dishwater. He might have been the first person to breathe it; it might have been made just for him.

While he was still enjoying the taste of the air he grew aware of sound: not the voice, which in his state of cloudy unconcern he had all but forgotten, but a low-pitched drone so unvarying in pitch and volume that he had difficulty discerning it – his brain told him to ignore it as he ignored his heartbeat, the sound of his breathing. It was not loud but nor was it distant: when he concentrated on it, it seemed to be all around him, barely within the range of his hearing, so low that he could feel it in his fingertips almost as well as he could hear it.

Thinking of his fingers reminded Dak that he had a body as well as senses. He tried to account for the feeling of unease which came with the appreciation but failed to, at least in time. Bracing the palm of one hand against the yielding surface beneath him he pushed himself on to his side and raised his head. With the movement both comfort and disorientation vanished. Pain, like from before but not so bad, forced his floating senses back into their usual association with his body and full consciousness returned.

The voice said, "Lie still and the pain will diminish."

Panting slightly, Dak eased himself back on to his face and in so doing saw for the first time the electrode attached to his wrist. He recognised what it was and its function without understanding what it was doing on him. Depending on whether or not the worm sequence had been a dream, he had expected to wake – if he woke at all – either back on board *Leviathan* or down on the surface of Terra. He had not expected to find himself in a hospital unit with machinery monitoring his vital signs and someone with a cold, toneless voice watching over him.

That voice again. It itself, rather than anything it said, twanged a chord in his memory. For a moment he had to reach for it; then it was his. His heart leapt, paused, and began to race. Careless of his pains he tried to lift his head and look around. "Where are you? Come where I can see you. Are you ashamed to face me?"

"I am here."

Weakness frustrated Dak's efforts. After a tremblingly short minute he was forced to concede his will to his rebel body and return his hot brow to the cool comfort of the shiny unpillowed bed. "Damn you," he muttered, lamentably close to tears.

"Do not distress yourself. You will be stronger soon. Your injuries are healing well. Soon we will talk."

But the short speech had given Dak a purchase. No one of his generation was unfamiliar with the subtle changes wrought in the human voice by electronic translation. "Wait," he said. His voice came raggedly, broken upon his stressed breathing. "Why are you lying to me? You're not here at all. All that's here is a – a voice-box. Where are you this time? Is this the closest I'm ever going to get to you?"

"Yes. Now sleep."

Somehow he had no choice.

When next he awoke he found himself on his back, the electrodes gone, and on a table by the bed a bowl of some substance he could not identify with a spoon stuck in it to show that it was food. Dak didn't remember eating since before his troubles started on *Leviathan*, which the state of his back argued must now be some time ago. But he didn't feel hungry so he supposed someone must have fed him in the interim. The white worm again tickled his memory.

He sat up without ill-effect, pushed the sheet off his legs and tried to stand. He found himself on his knees on the floor, a harder version of the same shiny plastic as the bed. Across the room a door opened to admit a soft clatter which struck a momentary chill at his heart. The pincer nose of the great white worm appeared round the end of the bed and before he had time to protest it curved itself around his waist and lifted him solicitously back to where he had started. Its skin was the same plastic as the bed, as the floor. For the first time objectively he realised that it was not a living creature but a mechanical, a tool of some kind. All the same it seemed very considerate of his welfare.

"Take your time, Dak Hamiko. You have not left that bed for a fortnight."

It was not the worm which spoke, but it might as well have been: there was no one else in the room. For a moment Dak resisted talking to an absentee host, but his curiosity was stronger than his resentment. "What is this place? How did I get here?"

"This is a bunker complex half a mile below the surface of Earth. I had you brought here by lander from the helium miner."

"*Leviathan*. What happened to her? – I had a friend on board."

"It is in orbit. It will remain so until you are ready to leave."

"Waiting for me? That doesn't sound very like Divik."

"Divik was the captain? The captain is dead."

In all honesty Dak could not deny himself a small sigh of relief. "So Sharm is in command."

"Your friend? A big man in black clothes?" Dak nodded. "He died also. A bolt from a laser pistol. The entire crew is dead. The vessel is unoccupied."

Dak stared up at the ceiling and the ceiling seemed to be spinning. He moaned aloud, a murmured grief. On the whole, perhaps, they had not been good men; but they had been men, too nearly divine to die of mere expedience. What they had done in fear should not have been paid in anger. His voice came out broken, and he didn't care or even notice. "You killed them – all? Why?"

"It was necessary."

"*Why?*"

"They would have killed you. It was necessary that you remain alive."

"Seventeen men –"

"Sixteen. They killed your friend Sharm. They would have killed you."

"No . . ."

"They would. As it was they left you to die."

Feeling sick, Dak closed his eyes and let his chin sink on his chest. "What happened?"

"I activated the primary warning system. In the belief that the flight-deck was depressurising they retreated to the technical area and closed the bulkhead. The captain shot your friend from the hatch as he withdrew. You were unconscious. If they had pulled you out of there, if any one of them had tried to save you, they would have survived. They did not. They sealed you in what they believed to be a punctured section. So I opened the airlock in the technical area and blew them into space."

Dak was appalled, as much by the speaker's cold acceptance of his actions as by the actions themselves. He had always wondered whether murder, which was by its nature passionate, were not a less terrible crime than execution, which was not. Divik had no reason to kill Sharm, yet that hot-blooded act of fury Dak could contemplate with only deep sorrow, while the considered judicial exercise of turning men out to their death among the stars filled him with horror and a kind of vicarious guilt. Not even so much because they had died, but because this other had killed, dispassionately.

In a low voice tremulous with bridled anger Dak said, "Whatever gave you the right to judge their lives less precious than mine?"

"My purpose. My purpose is paramount, and I need you to complete it."

"Purpose? Seventeen men are dead and you talk about a purpose? What can possibly be more important than the lives of seventeen men?"

"A nation, Dak Hamiko. A people."

"That's what you said in the messages."

"You said you did not understand."

"I still don't." The anger had gone, leaving him drained.

"But you will. I promise you that. I have waited a long time."

"Three months," Dak said uncertainly. He wasn't sure he understood the conversation. "Nearer four?"

"Four months!" The voice was rampant with scorn; it rattled in the hidden transceiver as if it were not made for, or at least not accustomed to, such vehemence. "Four months? You impose on me your own pitiful scale. What are four months to me? Or four years, or forty, or four hundred? I have been waiting for this time, Dak Hamiko, for millennia."

Dak's voice when it came seemed to issue from the bottom of a deep hole and only just reach the rim. "What are you?"

"I am the Matrix."

"Where are you?"

"Look around."

Jerkily, like a marionette, his body spastic with premonition, he did so. White plastic, everywhere, around and above and below – a timeless immutable vista of white plastic. Understanding reached for him with fingers like tendrils of smoke. "You are – this – building?"

"I am the computer intelligence governing this building and its function," said the Matrix, as if by rote. "I was created by men to do what they could not live long enough to do themselves. I am the custodian of their immortality."

Dak felt his head reel, heard the blood thunder in his ears, felt the worm press him anxiously back against the bed. The Matrix said, "Rest now. We will talk again later."

"Wait," said Dak, willing his pulse to steady and his voice to be calm. "I'm all right. Don't go."

"Go?" The Matrix seemed almost to chuckle. "Where do you suppose I can go? I'm not a robot, I'm a two billion cubic foot complex."

Lying back at the insistence of the worm – it had far too much personality for him to think of it as a machine – Dak closed his eyes and let the Matrix's words sink in. They sank, echoing and re-echoing through the vortices of his mind, forming patterns that he could almost see with his shut eyes – like the messages that he could almost understand, and the absurd train of events that had brought him here, and the people of half a dozen starships and settlements who didn't even know the show was playing, much less that they were playing in it. His mind spun with it all, inward and downward, faster and tighter, so that afterwards he could not be sure if he had spent moments or hours in the labyrinth of his psyche, but when the white plastic world came back he knew the next question, and he could have made a good stab at the answer.

"This – building. This complex. What is its function?"

He expected resistance, evasion, at least a dramatic pause. But the Matrix responded with an immediacy and a directness that underlined its inhumanity more than anything else could have. "I am a gene bank, an incubator and a cryogenic suspension chamber.

I am the womb that will people the earth, when the earth is ready."

It was green once (said the Matrix): a dozen different sorts of green, also blue, and brown, and golden and white; a world so perfect in its infinite variety that its children were fitted physically and psychologically to live and flourish in any conditions not actually poisonous to them. Nature's hand-crafted colonists, they went forth and seeded the galaxy with their strongest and their best. Forest world and desert worlds and ocean planets, and even one composed largely of glass: they discovered them, tamed them and found ways of being happy and prosperous on them.

Which was just as well, because when they went forth conquering and to conquer they left Earth at the mercy of her weaker and less noble sons. More than that, to reach the stars they had raped her, robbed her, stripped her of resources laid down before their own ancestors dropped from the trees. When they rode the silver flames towards their bright future under new suns they left behind a planet over-exploited and running down and a degenerate population already polarising in anticipation of want and famine and armed oppression of the weak and meek by the strong and bad. Local skirmishes over land developed into nationalistic wars which confounded sociologists, who thought mankind had evolved beyond such vulgarities. Within three generations there was no common civilisation on Earth, only a thousand disparate kingdoms under a thousand technocrats, jealous and bloody, each permanently armed against the others. They used laser-guided missiles and fission bombs instead of longbows and trebuchets, but otherwise there was little to choose between Earth after the Diaspora and Europe before Agincourt.

The termites squabbled savagely over whose territory began and ended where; meanwhile the tree was rotting. The fossil fuels had long since been exhausted. The island kingdoms became more and more dependent on nuclear power and less respectful of it, so that accidents were inevitable and increasingly frequent: all that happened when a warlord blew his atomic palace into the ionosphere was that the half-dozen whose lands bordered his moved in swiftly to grab a piece of the action. Radiation levels began to rise, not only because of fall-out but also because the ozone layer came under attack from airborne effluent. Thermal pollution, which had started during the twentieth century and received a massive boost from the myriad launchings of the Diaspora, finally closed the skylight on the greenhouse and after that there were no more blue skies, just a shimmering silver haze laced with chemical smoke, hot winds that turned farmland into dust and grassland into desert, and a tide which came higher every day.

Earth was dying on her feet, neither her human nor geological resources recycling, but there was a glimmer in the darkness and it was the minds of great men; for neither the sciences nor the humanities had entirely died or been totally perverted. Now they spoke together. The physicists said the surface of Earth was degenerating and would not support any but the most basic life-forms for more than a very few centuries. The sociologists made the physicists feel at first better and then worse: they concluded that it would not matter whether the planet continued unchanged for a thousand eons, because civilisations were themselves mortal and Earth's was in its death-throes. Biologists brought perhaps the bleakest news of all. Neither the increasing hostility of the environment nor the death of civilisation had any relevance beside the fact that mankind was changing, mutating, no longer breeding true. Freaks of nature had been recorded throughout history – Anne Boleyn had an extra finger – but these days there was no knowing what would issue from a woman's womb. The human, the nearly-human and the wholly unrecognisable: family likeness was now a matter of producing a child with the same quota of limbs as its parents.

It was not recorded who first raised the possibility of a gene-bank. It was inevitable, perhaps, that one of them should, given the technological brilliance of which they were capable and the grim, implacable force with which Nature drives her children to survive. It had not been tried before – utter catastrophe is seldom contemplated, much less taken as a working hypothesis – but many of the techniques had, and if they acted soon and together these great men could still command the necessary resources. They started work on the time-capsule. They buried it deep, against the most cataclysmic surface disturbances. They distilled genes from the healthiest of surviving strains, both intellectual and physical traits receiving due attention. Around them they built a machine, a machine capable of sampling the surface environment, of knowing when it would again sustain life, and then of converting coloured protoplasms in a gene-bank into people.

Halfway through the building they got cold feet, these great men. They realised that what they were doing had never been tried before, outside a laboratory, and decided to take out insurance against some unforeseen factor rendering the entire project a failure. To the gene-bank and its attendant machine they added a cryogenic suspension unit complete with *its* attendant machine, where strong young bodies in varying stages of maturity lay in frozen tanks waiting through centuries of winter for the ultimate spring.

And then it was realised that, whether born or thawed, the new people would not emerge from their chrysalides fit and ready to conquer a world. There would have to be a period of adjustment, a time of learning, and they would need to be protected while they learned. So living quarters were incorporated into the machine, together with a distillation of all the knowledge gained during ten thousand years of civilisation; graded, so that the new people should not be smothered with information, drowned in it, and the harder parts to understand – like why they were there at all – reserved until the simpler concepts had been mastered. About this time they started calling the machine the Matrix.

And they did all this without knowing, and in the certainty that they would never know, whether Earth could ever again support higher life-forms; and if it could, whether the Matrix would fulfil its myriad tasks without fatal flaw, whether the mathematics of the laboratory would be borne out by practical results, or whether the genes themselves carried locked within them the seeds of their own destruction. They did not know. There was no way they could know. They devoted their failing energies and their final resources to the construction of the Matrix as the supreme statement of

34

human optimism.

Dak sat curled around his thoughts, hugging bony knees to his chest, a maelstrom of conflicting emotions whirling within him. He was not entirely aware that the Matrix had stopped speaking. He no longer felt faint but the giddiness remained: he seemed to be the one still point at the centre of a spinning room and beyond that a spinning world, a spinning galaxy, a spinning universe. He felt the worm nuzzle his hand; it was probably trying to monitor his pulse but instinctively and without thinking he patted its head.

The Matrix spoke again, reproof in its metallic tones. "I was correct. You were not ready to assimilate this information. I should have waited until you were stronger."

Dak forced himself to come to terms with the situation, however superficially. He had to cough twice to find a voice he recognised as his own. "I doubt it would have made much difference. Surely you didn't expect me to absorb all that without some reaction?"

"No," conceded the Matrix. "I expected that at first you would not believe."

Dak nodded slowly, finding comfort in the rhythm and relief for overtense muscles. He realised he had been locked in that foetal position for a very long time and made a conscious effort to relax, drawing the pure air deep into his constricted lungs. "Yet a blanket refusal to believe would have been irrational. If what you say is not at least substantially true, why would you trouble to tell it to me? Why would you bring me here at all? Why would you exist? I'd need an alternative truth before I could challenge yours. So far I have none.

"All the same," he added, his brow clouding as the riptide of his thoughts swirled across the foreshore of his synapses, leaving a tangled wrack of ideas, "why did you bring me here?"

"Sufficient unto the day," said the Matrix, exhibiting its classical education. "We shall discuss that later, when you have adjusted to the position I have described. For the moment it is enough to say that I require your assistance with a small detail of my programmed function and you will not be detained long."

"That's all right," said Dak, responding with automatic politeness to an agency he could not help thinking of as more human than mechanical, "I have nowhere else to go."

Later he returned to *Leviathan*, still in a holding orbit beyond the turbulent atmosphere. The Matrix did not seem entirely happy about his request but nor was it prepared to refuse it. The landing-craft remained on remote control; Dak was offered no instruction in its use. The white worm which accompanied him was both an aide and at least tacitly a warder. The inference, unstated but unmistakable, was that Dak had the freedom of Earth but not yet the freedom to leave it.

The sombre purpose of his journey – to consign to eternity the body of his friend – did not wholly eclipse his interest in it. It was, after all, his first sight of the planet of his ancestors. When he had passed this way before, brought from *Leviathan* to the Matrix, he had seen nothing.

He found the lander sitting on its tail in a vertical shaft well away from the main complex. The shaft was sunk through solid rock to shield the Matrix from heat and vibration, and only a corridor from the upper levels penetrated the shock barrier. The vehicle was a stubby little thing with a blunt nose and a broad bottom, the main engines packed into the stern section, a circlet of manoeuvring jets around its ample belly. A catwalk reached out from the hatch at the end of the corridor to one in the side of the lander. As Dak stepped out over the shaft the air changed abruptly, from the pure synthetic stuff generated by the Matrix to something hot and dry and heavy with dust. Coughing, he looked up. Far above his head the shaft ended in a clear-cut circle of thunder-grey laced with fast-moving khaki which he did not immediately recognise as the sky.

Even for a young man of his generation Dak was well travelled. He had travelled on luxury star liners and on grubby tramps which made *Leviathan* look glamorous. But the brief minutes which it took for the lander to claw its way up through the raging atmosphere, fighting successively clear of the roiling surface sandstorms, the streaking winds and the towering systems of turbulence which stood between the launch shaft and the dark haven of peace and silence beyond the ionosphere, were among the most uncomfortable of his unconventional life. He was accustomed to hoverflight for surface travel and star drive for crossing the stellar void: he was not used to riding a double-jointed camel, and nothing else could have prepared him for the nightmare of surge, swoop and tumble which waited beyond the rim of the shaft. Unacquainted with the concept of motion sickness, his first thought was that the monstrous buffeting had damaged the little craft and it was losing pressure; his second that the buffeting had damaged him and his guts, torn away from their retaining ligaments, were sloshing around in his abdominal cavity; and after that he thought nothing lucid until he came round to find the worm wiping his face with a damp cloth. His fingers were clenched like talons in the arms of his seat, and *Leviathan* was hoving into sight in the monitor above his head.

"Contrary to any impression you may be gaining," he muttered to the worm, extracting his fingernails from the upholstery, "I do not usually faint this easily, or this often."

"Syncope," responded the worm promptly, in a voice exactly similar to that of the Matrix, "is a natural reaction to stresses beyond the subject's capacity to cope."

Dak, thinking himself alone, had startled at the sound. He eyed the sinuous white member suspiciously. "I didn't know you could talk."

"I am the Matrix," the worm said with familiar pomposity, and the lander jarred slightly as it docked with *Leviathan*.

Nothing aboard the helium miner had changed. Sharm lay as Dak had last seen him, before the worm pulled him into the darkness: a large mound on the floor of the flight-deck clad in black with silver studs. In life the studs had been a part of him, together with the massive frame, the brusque manner, the power that radiated from him. In the stillness of death they appeared an affectation. The body, preserved by the chill of space, bore little resemblance to the man Dak had known. It seemed gross, vain and smugly censorious from its refuge beyond mortality. Sharm had been none of those things. It came as a small revelation to Dak, changing grief to sorrow and absorbing sorrow into the great pool of human experience, so that he could look at the body with wonder in his eyes and something like a smile and say, "There's nothing of him here." The worm had the sense not to reply.

With the worm's help Dak coffined Sharm's body in a torpedo shell which he loaded into *Leviathan*'s main cannon. He fired it directly at the earth and watched until it reached the atmosphere and burned up in a moment's brilliance.

In the plastic warren below he had no way of judging time, but after some of it had elapsed he asked the Matrix, "If you won't tell me why you brought me here, will you tell me how?"

The Matrix preened in a wholly unmechanical fashion. "No great feat, for a computer. We understand one another far better than the men who build us. It was easy enough for me to tap into the central telegraphic computer and have the messages sent to your hotels. Similarly the video-call on Ganymede. Arranging for your arrest was equally simple. It occurred to me that *Leviathan* might refuse to take you however eloquent your pleas." It seemed to Dak that the Matrix was squinting at him sideways. "I communicated to the InterPol computer an entirely fictitious record of your crimes. I said you liked sleeping with small children. I was torn, momentarily, between small children and dead bodies, but on the whole the former seems to elicit the greater indignation.

"Anyway, IpCom did the rest. It never occurred to the police on Ganymede to question information from InterPol central records, so they deported you – aboard the only suitable vessel then in the spaceport. The last stages of *Leviathan*'s flight I manipulated by direct contact with the onboard computer."

"You've quite an old boys' act going, haven't you, you computers?" Dak had by no means forgiven the murder of the miner's crew, and he wasn't exactly thrilled by this new information regarding his criminal record. "How did you stop *Leviathan*?"

"A tractor beam, converting the ship's velocity into planetary angular momentum. Do you understand physics?"

"Not the way you mean," Dak said in a low voice.

"Then there's no point my telling you any more than that the energy taken from the ship was absorbed into the planet's revolution.

Clear?"

"Crystalline. But I'm not here – at least I don't suppose I'm here – for elementary instruction in thermodynamics. Why am I here?"

Slipping smoothly into an evasive mode, the Matrix chose to misunderstand him. "I brought you here," it said, emphasising the penultimate word fractionally but not by accident, "because of all the millions of people on whom information was available to me you seemed the most suitable for my purpose. I needed someone who was free to come here, who could be persuaded to come, and who would follow my instructions once here."

"Useless, stupid and malleable," Dak paraphrased coldly.

"On the contrary." The Matrix sounded genuinely surprised. "If that were my requirement I need have sent no farther than Security Centre on Ganymede, where I could have had a wide choice. No. I needed someone of intelligence, integrity, insight. I needed someone of understanding and compassion, someone of humanity. I chose you."

"Flattery will get you nowhere," Dak said flatly. "Even were we to accept that I am this paragon of all the old-fashioned virtues, you haven't explained how you found me."

"By your poetry."

"You read poetry?"

"I have access to all matter committed to computer memory banks within range of my receptors; which is effectively the civilised galaxy. Every printed work is fed into central archives, which occupy virtually the whole of a major moon in Antares. Your poetry suggested you as a likely subject, other material about you reinforced the hypothesis, so I made contact. I sent the messages."

"I told you, I didn't understand the messages."

"No. But you responded to them."

"All right. You found me and you got me here. Now what?"

"Now," said the Matrix with artificial bonhomie, "I'm going to treat you to a picture show."

Dak caught himself breathing heavily, controlled it. "I outgrew Saturday matinees when I was nine. I don't want pictures, I want answers."

"Perhaps the pictures will give you some answers. As you have pointed out more than once, I have brought you a long way. The least I can do is show you where you are."

"The least you can do is tell me why."

"That comes next. For the moment – behold, the planet Earth."

The light went out, leaving Dak briefly in a black limbo. He felt his balance just beginning to waver when another and different light sprang up from a different but equally untraceable source near the floor and illuminated a wall. The wall came alive with colours. He was looking at a plant. In the heart of the plant was a flower, and on the rim of the flower was an insect, wings a shimmer of speed. The plant receded slowly. There was movement under its fringing leaves and a small furry face quested the air momentarily before withdrawing behind the rustling curtain.

The picture tore up and reformed as a forest. Dense vegetation crowded out the sky. Quick movements and flashes of colour in the high foliage betrayed the presence of birds. There was no soundtrack: Dak heard in his own head the raucous cries that go with vivid plumage.

After the forest there was a timbered copse, a riot of flowering shrubs and, beyond, pasture plunging into a valley of water-meadows. Trees wept over their own reflections in a meandering stream, rushes whispered conspiratorially.

Dak began to get a very strange feeling about it all. "This is Earth? Now?"

"Only recently," allowed the Matrix. "And only limited areas. For an epoch the land was incapable of supporting any stable regenerating eco-system. Even now the conditions which produce this kind of response exist only in certain singular zones. But those zones can be extended."

"There was no sand."

"Earth is not covered entirely by sand."

"From space it appears to be virtually cocooned in dust storms. I should have expected at least a dust haze."

"You would have been mistaken," said the Matrix briskly, and Dak's strange feeling grew. He asked to see the tape again. The

Matrix said it would take time to rewind.

"Besides which," it added, "the moment has arrived for you to understand why you are here."

"You have decided to complete your task."

"You guessed that?"

"What else could you need help with? What else have you to do?"

"You are disconcerting company, Dak Hamiko. You draw inferences faster than a computer."

"Used responsibly, we humans have our place."

"Ah," said the Matrix. "Satire."

"You still haven't explained what you want me for. You are, after all," said Dak, with more than a trace of malice, "the Matrix, the final brilliant flowering of a doomed culture. How could you possibly need the services of a wandering poet?"

The Matrix had little sense of humour and no capacity for laughing at itself. "I should have thought," it said, in a tone of quiet reproof, "that with a people awaiting your pleasure to be born, you would have more important things on your mind than scoring off me."

Dak refused to be chastened by a machine. "If you see yourself as the mother of men, you had better learn that nose-thumbing in the face of the awesome is the human divinity. So stop being so pompous and tell me what went wrong with you."

The Matrix was scandalised. Lacking the experience in polemic which would have enabled it to respond as an affronted man would, it fell into a kind of aggrieved mechanical stammer. "I am the Matrix, I am –"

"You're a splendid panjandrum and an example to us all," Dak said soothingly, "but unless something had gone wrong with you, you wouldn't be seeking my help. By the same token, it can't be anything serious or you'd have chosen someone considerably more practical than a man to whom screwdriver is an eleven-letter word with virtually no poetic uses. On the basis of all the available evidence, I conclude that you've blown a fuse."

There was a short assimilatory pause as the Matrix adjusted to the unexpected flippancy. Its makers had been serious men in a grim situation, they had seen no reason to imbue their creation with wit; and nothing in the solemn golden-smooth face of the young man Dak Hamiko warned of this strain of levity. Yet the Matrix was a sophisticated instrument, capable of subtle and complex feats of learning, and in time it could learn to answer satire with satire. It said, "I did not choose you for your engineering erudition. The solution to my dilemma is ludicrously simple. Access to my circuits is by means of a central shaft. Near the top is a blue button. It requires to be pressed. That is all."

"I don't understand. If you know what's wrong and how to fix it, why haven't you?"

"Anything else and I could have done." The Matrix sounded resentful. "In every other respect I am self-regenerating. I can replace everything from a printed circuit to an exhausted plutonium rod. But men made me, and being men they made me imperfect. They built in a fail-safe mechanism, and the fail-safe mechanism failed.

"They were afraid that I might make a mistake and wake the people before the world was ready for them. There would only ever be one chance: if they awoke too soon they would die and the dream would be over." Dak smiled to himself. From talking with a poet the Matrix had learned the art of poesy. If Dak had been a soldier it would by now have been talking in terms of stratagems and personnel.

"So they installed a fail-safe device, an independent circuit to which I as the Matrix did not have access, to detect any reckless haste on my part. If this device found me preparing to activate the arousal systems before it was safe to do so it was to cut in and stop me: not for that moment alone, but for ever. The decision would be taken out of my hands. The people would stay asleep until the earth drew others from outside, who would complete the circuit. I did not wish to trust to the first comers having noble motives. So I brought you."

"The fail-safe device malfunctioned?"

"It did. It misinterpreted a standard sampling check as a move towards arousal, noted that external conditions were still

42

unfavourable for human survival, and shut down on that final phase of my capability which gave point to all the rest. That was three thousand years ago. Since then I have maintained the cryogenic chamber and the gene-bank and monitored the environment as before; but with the knowledge that when the time came I would need help. The time has come. You have come. The waiting is over."

"For lo," Dak said softly, "the winter is past. The rain is over and gone. The flowers appear on the earth. The time of the singing of birds is come, and the voice of the turtle is heard in our land."

After a moment the Matrix said, "Did you write that?"

"No," admitted Dak; "and I don't for one minute believe that Solomon did either."

The Matrix showed him the cryogenic chamber. Because of the radically low temperature it was not possible for him to enter, but there was an observation gallery from which he gazed spellbound over a glimmering crystal field of uncountable, identical translucent chests; row on row of them, like coffins after an air disaster, but with an alien purity, untouched by human hands; at least this side of eternity. The Matrix said that the chamber, in all its vastness, was but one of eight.

The gene-bank was – bizarre reaction! – more fun. The coloured distillates were only chemicals, not people: Dak did not feel for them the same sense of responsibility, the same fearful urgency, that the crystal boxes with their frozen, eons-old children invoked in him.

A small emergency arose somewhere in the far reaches of the complex and, with a click which could have been a mechanical swear-word, the Matrix left. Not physically, of course; physically it was as omnipresent as always, but its silicon attention was diverted elsewhere. Dak spoke its name a couple of times, loudly, without any reaction. He supposed that if he were to stage an emergency of his own that attention would revert to this sector, but routine and trivia were being ignored while the Matrix tackled the problem, whatever it was. There was no way of knowing how long it would take. Dak resolved to make the most of it.

He had not at that time any clearly formed notion that the

Matrix was deceiving him, only a niggling doubt that he had not been told all there was to know. Without knowing how far he would be allowed to proceed he set out to explore, hurrying but trying not to run for fear of drawing notice on himself. It was for all the world, he thought with a grin, like stealing fruit from the orchards of Tok-ai-Do when he was a boy; and he hadn't been much good at that, either.

He expected his first and fundamental problem to be how he would open doors – presupposing that he could recognise them in the white plastic warren of the blind corridors. He had no such difficulties. Doors were clearly delineated by a coloured frame; apart from the gene bank the only colour he had seen in the complex. The colours varied through a handful of options, but if it were a code he did not yet understand it. The doors opened if he stood in front of them. He passed soon into regions he had not yet glimpsed.

He found the hospital wing. It was much larger, of course, than the single room in which he woke after the dying aboard *Leviathan*. There was a faint plastic rattle as the servitor which had nursed him raised its head enquiringly. He greeted it quietly, as a man arriving home late at night might reassure his dog before it should rouse the household, and it subsided. Beyond the hospital he found lecture halls, dining-rooms, community rooms; all cold, clinical, unused from their construction. The vast white empty rooms struck a chill at him that had nothing to do with the temperature. He moved faster, taking no account of where he was going, knowing he could not be lost for any longer than it took the Matrix to deal with its problem and come seeking him: He was not, after all, close to the Matrix. He was within it.

A door opened on green. The sudden colour, after days in a white world, was dazzling. It stopped him in his tracks; and while the colour filled his eyes, the scent filled his nostrils, vulnerable from the long lack of stimulation. The scent, too, was green: deep vibrant green, bright virile green, and the dark brown of damp earth. The smell was almost too good to be true. It was the smell of things living and growing in this sterile wilderness beneath the hostile surface of a ravaged land. Dak stepped into the Matrix's greenhouse.

The light source was a battery of solar lamps far above his head, but most of them he could not see except as a warm yellow glow filtering through leaves and dappling the ground with brightness. Of the roof beyond the lamps he could see nothing. The only ceiling he knew was the green one, spreading in variegated planes from the boles of mighty trees. He had not seen trees since leaving home. Like a child in its first forest he wandered aimless and enthralled, feeling the roughness of bark with his fingertips, the veined smoothness of a leaf, the spring of humus under his bare feet, until he had no idea where the door lay. His eyes were filled with verdure, he was filled with the song of the trees, the whispering rhythm of their poetry.

"'Fresh groves grow up, and their green branches shoot towards the old and still enduring skies,'" Dak quoted reverently. Then, the glory of it welling up through him, he shouted it out loud and went running among the stout columns until his strength, but lately recovered, gave out and left him sweating and out of breath, sprawled in the fibrous arms of an inviting root-system.

A few yards away across the forest floor a flowering plant sent a silent cascade of foliage to the ground. Among the leaves was a sudden movement, and a small furry face quested the air momentarily before withdrawing behind the rustling curtain.

When the Matrix came looking, it found Dak still in the same position, as if frozen there. His face was fixed in hard, unnatural lines and his eyes, when he raised them from the shrub, blazed dark in anger and resentment.

The Matrix took the offensive. "You should not be here. This is a restricted area."

"You lied to me." Dak's voice was low and thick with accusation.

"This is a controlled eco-system which could be destroyed by careless –"

"You lied to me. There are no forests, no fertile places. Not out there. Only here. No birds. No animals, no trees. Only a wind-blown desert. Like Sharm said."

"The atmosphere is carefully filtered. The introduction of bacteria or viruses harmless in a normal environment could do profound damage –"

"Damn your pathetic little experiments!" Dak came to his feet in one fast, flowing movement like a hunting cat. "Don't you understand, I *know*. No wonder you wouldn't show me the video again. It was shot in here: the only place on this God-forsaken planet where there are trees and life and no dust. They have nowhere to go, have they? You want me to wake these poor children to a life within your plastic boundaries. Why? Did you get bored with being alone? Wasn't playing with people on distant systems enough for you? Did you want real live dolls that you could hold? You're sick. Thank God for the fail-safe!"

There was a long pause before the Matrix spoke again. "You are distraught," it said then, coldly. "I do not know why but you are obviously upset. For that reason I will overlook your manner on this occasion. But I must ask you to remember: I am the Matrix. I am the law here. You will not be permitted disrespect."

Dak gaped. "You megalomaniac clutter of nuts and bolts! You're a machine – oh, a very fine one I don't doubt, but still only a machine. Men made you, and they were clever enough to impose on you a restraint that you are not clever enough to circumvent. You think you can bring me here, by force, manipulating and murdering as you please, feed me a tale of woe supported by a doctored video-tape, and I'll push your little buttons and touch my forelock to you and never know I've been taken for a ride? My friend, you don't understand men as well as you think you do. Oh, we have our faults, we're weak and often silly, and we have an absurdly keen awareness of our own dignity, but, on the whole, we are not overawed by mere might, either physical of intellectual. You can't bully me into doing what you want, and you patently can't force me – the fail-safe will stop you. Waiting for me for millennia, were you? Well, you'll have to wait a few millennia more, because I agree with the failsafe. This planet is not ready for these people. I won't press your damn button."

He turned and stalked away; away, at least, from the conversation

– the Matrix was, as ever, all around him. He took three strides; then pain hit him, from behind, washing over him like a wave. For a scant moment it held him immobile; then it left and let him stumble to his hands and knees, moaning faintly.

"I am sorry – I regret deeply –" stammered the Matrix. "Your back – I forgot. Let me help you –"

"Leave me alone," Dak mumbled, hunched up foetally on the floor. The pain was gone but the memory of it was shocking. After a minute, with the jelly in his knees beginning to set, he made it to his feet. He straightened up. "I mean it," he said, and his voice was dead. "I won't be the one to complete your circuit. I wouldn't give you a dog to play with, much less a nation of new-born children. Kill me if you choose, but I won't do it. You can't make me."

Chapter Three

The Matrix, in a fit of fury and frustration, began by trying to make him. As he had supposed, it was unable physically to force him to do the required work – it was a fundamental part of the fail-safe mechanism to ensure that it could not – but there were other methods at its disposal. When Dak returned to his quarters he found that the dispensing machine had been disconnected, leaving him without food or water. He was confined to his room, not by locked doors but by a sheet of the same pain stimulus which hit him when he tried to leave. The temperature in the room began to vacillate wildly from sub-polar to supra-equatorial: the sweat which poured from him one moment froze him the next. Presently he stopped sweating.

Water arrived. He drank it. He meant to save some for later but he couldn't stop drinking until it was gone. More came almost immediately, then none for a long time; after that he didn't know when it came, only that when it came he drank it. With no other means of monitoring time he came to take the period between drinks as a standard unit, which it was not. An equally random ratio between light and darkness in his cell contributed to the breakdown of reality. So did intermittent periods of white sound pumped through the walls.

He began to hallucinate. At first he knew that the bright colours and moving shadows were only figments of his abused senses. Later he was aware of nothing but the colours and shades and the denizens, massive and monstrous, of that dream-plane. He could not hear himself shouting and did not know what he was saying; but the Matrix did. The sounds of his anguish beat through its silicon brain until its anger gave way to sorrow and something akin to contrition. "I am a man," he screamed, "I am a man;" and he screamed it until his voice wore down to a croak.

The Matrix stopped tormenting him and started talking to him. At first, in his disorientation, Dak didn't know what it was saying, its words were only part of the general confusion of sensations coruscating in his synapses, but later as equilibrium returned he was able to understand.

"Yes, I did deceive you," it said. "I made the video, as you surmised, in the dendrosphere, not on the surface. The surface is recovering, but slowly – there are no forests, but there is ground cover and there are places where the heath is beginning to be colonised by sturdy low shrubs. There will be trees. And once there are trees the dust storms will stop – grind to a halt. Even the shrubs are helping to slow them down, taking some of the force out of them. There are places now where a man could live carefully.

"But that's not what I want for my people. They won't have that kind of expertise, the inborn knack of survival. No, for the first few generations they'll live here, in the complex, and go out to work on the surface. I have all the facilities they will need. I can keep them safe, and with my technology they can carve from the wilderness a new Eden for their children's children.

"Sapling trees from the dendrosphere will be transplanted outside. That will give them a windbreak to work behind, and when the trees are established the rains will come. Rain will settle the dust and make it loam; new growth will bind it to the earth. It's rich, fertile: there is nothing it won't grow, given water. When the dust storms stop, forests and grassland will spread with nothing to check them. The grandchildren of the people you saw in the cryogenic chamber will inherit a virgin world.

"Dak, Dak, can't you of all people appreciate what a thing it will be, to restore life to a desert planet? It's not just impatience which impels me to start the arousal. I don't think the regenerative process can be completed without human help; not, at least, within the foreseeable future. And there may be a time limit.

"Men like your friend Sharm and his crew are waking up to the possibilities of mining suns like Sol. For the moment they confine themselves to gathering helium. But the technology exists and could soon be widely available to take more than the mere waste-products of natural reactions. They could soon be exploiting the very substance of the sun itself. When that happens, it will be suns whose planets support no intelligent life whose death warrants will be signed by the Alliance. Sol is an obvious candidate. The spaceport on Ganymede will be transferred elsewhere – it is anyway out of date and under-used. And when the sun stops shining I will stop, and the suspended and potential lives of my people will stop. But if I can have a viable community of Earthmen living and working here by then, the Alliance will protect them. The miners will be sent elsewhere."

"Why not seek the protection of the Alliance now?" asked Dak.

"They are too vulnerable. Any decision could be made about them in which they would have no voice. They could be moved elsewhere – it is doubtful if I could withstand the might of the Alliance without risking the destruction of my charge. They could be experimented upon – aroused not to the human life I was designed to give them but to some laboratory situation. There is no knowing what might become of them if the programme on which this entire project was based thousands of years ago is abandoned. I fear for them, Dak Hamiko!"

"So do I," said Dak. "You are afraid that those who may replace you will not have the wisdom or the integrity to deal with them compassionately. I am afraid that you may not."

He walked on the surface of Earth, suspended between three elements. Underfoot was sand, or it may have been mud, wet and hard and so smooth that it gave the illusion of being faintly domed. The filtered sunlight, red and exhausted from fighting its way through the dense roiling clouds, gleamed off the slick flank of the mud ahead, constant as a moontrack on water.

There was water too, on his left as he walked, the turgid and surf-laced rim of an ocean snapping for his heels. He had never seen so much water. It shone dully, like a battle-cruiser, with white glints where the wind had ripped off the surface and torn it to shreds. The shreds stung his face and hurt viciously when they got into his eyes. When he first found the ocean he thought the spray would blind him, but though his eyes itched and ached from it his vision, such as it was in the dim world, was unaffected.

The third element was the wind. Monstrous, unrelenting, it streamed by on all sides like an invisible army charging, trampling over him, making him fight for his ground. It was an onslaught full of sound, screaming and howling, sucking up the sounds of the ocean, tearing from his mouth any sound Dak made; so that after the first minutes, when he thought the maelstrom cacophony would drive him mad, he ceased to hear it in any objective way; almost, the sound of the wind became another element.

Moving automatically now, unaware of his own tiredness, Dak trudged through a cold, dark, hostile limbo, continually fighting for breath and having it knocked from him, and filled to the heart with the thrill of walking on the planet of his ancestors. It occurred to him to ask the Matrix where Japan was but logic said there was no point: the only bonsai trees and formal gardens now were on Tok-ai-Do, while all that remained of Japan was probably the cindery upper slopes of Fujiyama.

The Matrix had gone on arguing at him – not with him, because he had been too tired to join in – until he thought his brain would burst with all the words being fired at it. Finally, in desperation and with the faint hope of startling the Matrix into silence for a few blessed moments, he said, "If this Earth is such a marvellous place for your people, let me see for myself. Put me out on the surface and let me see what they'd have to cope with."

He thought it a constructive suggestion for three reasons. If Earth was the hell-hole Sharm said, the Matrix would have to admit it and that might be an end of it. If it was the potential Eden the Matrix said, Dak would happily press its little button and let the people wake. Or of the Matrix let him outside and it was still a hell-hole, he might not come back and that, too, would be an end of it. He was so depressed by now that each solution seemed of approximately equal merit.

The Matrix hummed and hawed for some considerable time – Dak left it to it and got some sleep – before finally agreeing to let him outside the complex. It produced for him a suit of protective clothing, with an intercom in the helmet, told him to stay within sight of the surface installations and return immediately when told, then reluctantly accompanied him to the main hatch.

When the doors closed behind him the Matrix felt lonely.

In the airlock Dak tried to gather his thoughts. It seemed likely he was going into some danger, and certain that he was not in the best shape either mentally or physically to cope with it. Part of him was altogether past caring, but in his core where he was not battle-fatigued the resilient spark of humanity continued to glow, that marvellous childlike ability to thrill to the strange and new, and at the insistent hammering of the wind beyond the hatch the ember quickened and flared, and he stepped out onto the surface with trepidation, excitement and joy.

Before he had time to orientate, the wind, heavy with sand, caught him and flung him against a corner of the building. He grunted in surprise and the Matrix filled his helmet with a babble of anxious questions.

By leaning on the wind as on a solid plane he found he could keep his balance, though walking was hard. He wondered if he should have accepted the Matrix's offer of transport, but still felt that the only way he would get the measure of Earth, learn its foibles, its meanness and its generosities, was face to face, on his own two feet, alone. He staggered out of the lee of the building and looked around.

The single-storey surface installation projected through a desolate plain in which bands of scrubby heathland, the short wiry grass pressed flat by the never-ending wind, alternated with long drifts of sand. The ripping air was full of sand, it danced like a wave across the flattened turf and, like a wave, broke against the Matrix's ancient, pristine walls in a welter of disordered particles. On the windward side the walls were piled high with drift. So far as Dak could see, which admittedly was not far in the livid twilight, there was no tree of any description, however low, gnarled or scrubby.

Nor could he imagine one prevailing against the abrasive bludgeon of the wind.

Dak walked around the surface block. It was quite small, bearing no relation to the complex below, and he doubted if it would be visible a hundred feet up in the crashing sky. He began to move away. At once the Matrix called him with renewed injunctions not to lose sight of the complex, not to risk losing his sense of direction, not to walk so far with the wind at his back that he'd have difficulty returning in the teeth of it.

"Tell me," said Dak, "is this semi-solid air breathable?"

"Certainly," said the Matrix; then, suspiciously, "Why?"

"Because if I can't switch you off I can at least remove you from immediate proximity to my ear." The last he heard was a protesting squawk as he took the helmet off.

The wind struck him in the mouth like a blow from a fist, tearing into his throat and lungs with its burden of sand and bringing tears to his eyes. After the pure, perfectly balanced, impotent cocktail inside it smelled like chemical soup, thick and pungent, and tasted of salt. Tunnelling upstream into it he found the sea and the slick wet beach where blown spray knocked the sand out of the air.

There occurred one of those sudden, inexplicable breaks in the cloud which Sharm had described. All in an instant the sky opened, bright sunlight flooded the storm-swept shore and the steely sea turned to lapis shot with lace. The profound unlooked for beauty of it stopped Dak in mid-stride.

The helmet swinging from his hand began babbling for attention. "The sun's just come out," he told it, marginally aware that the combination of tiredness and enchantment made him sound drunk.

"I know," the Matrix said tersely. "Come home now."

"The sun's come out. It's turned the sea to cobalt and the sand to red-gold. You should see it."

"I can see it. Come back inside."

"Not yet. I like it here with the sun on it."

"You are not the only one. At least leave the beach –"

As it spoke the sea beyond the surf erupted in a welter of foam and flesh as something huge and silver-grey, like a blunt and wrinkled torpedo powering up from the depths, burst through the squally surface in an arc that took it all but clear of the water before it came crashing back with an explosion of sound which carried even above the wind.

"What by all the fires of Phaeton was that?" gasped Dak, momentarily forgetting the wind which seized the chance to send him sprawling back on the mud.

"Dak, get out of there," yelled the tinny voice in the helmet.

Afterwards he had only a fleeting impression of agile grey cables rushing up the beach towards him, the avid clammy slap as the foremost clutched at his ankle, the intelligent hooded eyes in the bald beaky skull which rose from the water hard by the shore, and then adrenalin flooding his system as with panic driving his limbs and the wind at his back he fled for his life, the protective suit shredded to his knee and blood oozing from half a dozen small, perfectly circular lacerations in his leg. He fetched up at the top of the beach in time to see the helmet which he had dropped in his fright disappear below the surf in the grasp of those sinuous grey tentacles. Of the great head there was no longer a sign.

The Matrix, horrified by the sounds issuing from the intercom, immediately despatched the surface vehicle Dak had declined, its armament on remote control. It found him sitting on the turf at the edge of the beach, bareheaded, chin in hands, oblivious of his wounds, staring with total absorption at the vivid ocean which boiled with the richness of life brought up by the sun.

Back in the complex, the Matrix was both angry and defensive. As Dak sat patiently while the worm attended to his leg, it berated him energetically and illogically in the manner peculiar to mothers whose children have been in danger: You risk hurting yourself again and I'll flay you! Dak took it all philosophically, only filling the breathless gaps with his own observations.

"I told you to stay close by," ranted the Matrix. "I told you to return at once if I called you. Do you think that out there is a thrills dome in a pleasure palace? Do you think those things were laid on for your amusement, and would have short-circuited if you couldn't get out of the way? That squid wouldn't, he'd have chewed you up, swallowed you down and never even belched. It's a miracle you weren't killed."

"It must have teeth or something on the insides of the suckers," said Dak, looking with interest at the neatly chiselled roundels in his flesh.

"Never mind what it's got inside its suckers, it very nearly had you inside its gut. Why are men so stubborn? I told you to come off the beach, I told you it wasn't safe, but would you listen? No, you're just like the rest of them, puny and dim and convinced you know best. And where should I have been if it had got you? – back to square one, that's where, searching the Alliance for someone bright enough to follow instructions while my poor people go on sleeping with no dawn in sight. If you don't care about yourself or me, I'd have thought you would have more consideration for them."

"That ocean must be an ever-lasting Sunday lunch to grow things that size," mused Dak.

"Another performance like that and you'll be on the menu! When I heard water bubbling in the microphone I – my heart – hurt." The machine fumbled ineptly with the unfamiliar emotions. "That beach is a death-trap when the sun is on the water. Did you think I was exaggerating the danger? Did you think you, who've been here the wink of an eye, knew better than I, who have been here for eons?"

"You sound like my grandmother," grinned Dak. "Stop tearing strips off me and tell me about those creatures."

"I don't expect there are many of them," said the Matrix, suddenly guarded, after a pause.

"Of course there are. The sea was alive with them. Oh, I see – you think I won't wake the people to a life threatened by monsters. On the contrary. There's hardly a monster in the universe that men haven't either come to terms with, conquered or learned to avoid. No, the significance of those splendid creatures is first that they survived at all, i.e. the sea at least never died, and secondly that so many of them grow to such great size. If the oceanic eco-system can feed that lot, it can certainly feed a few thousand men. Whatever happens, they won't starve."

"Then you'll wake them."

Dak in turn fell silent. "I'll think about it," he said carefully after a tense minute. "As best I can. I promise."

He kept his promise. He thought so long and hard about it that the Matrix began to grow anxious for him. He hardly ate or slept, could not be drawn into conversation and took to spending long hours outside, walking in the wind.

Finally he came inside. He looked different. Struggle with the harsh environment had put new muscle on the long bones, the golden skin had darkened and grown coarse from exposure to the elements, the sun had put flecks in his eyes and the wind had put creases around them. In his time on Earth he had come to manhood.

Without bothering to strip off his protective suit he walked through the complex, down to the lower levels and the observation deck over the cryogenic chamber. His eyes fixed on the crystal chests, he addressed the Matrix in a voice quiet and somehow flat.

"All right, this is the bottom line. I want to go home. Send me back to Tok-ai-Do. I want to talk to my father about this. I promise to tell no one else, and I promise my father will tell no one. Whatever I decide as a result of that, I'll come back – to do as you ask, or to explain why I can't. It will be up to you, then, whether or not you let me leave."

The Matrix sent a team up to *Leviathan*, still blindly orbiting, to equip it for its forthcoming journey. It was the kind of team which did not require teabreaks or evenings off, but even so the work took time. While it progressed, far below in the heart of the Matrix the only two conscious, sentient beings on Earth – the one carbon based, the other silicon – talked long, quietly and without acrimony. The Matrix asked about Dak's father.

Dak smiled. "He's a good man. Not, perhaps, one of the Alliance's great minds, and he has no ear for music, but if you were to judge a man by honesty and integrity rather than achievement you'd go a long way to find his better. I love him very much."

"Is he Japanese too?"

"No. His forebears were European. He went to Tok-ai-Do as an irrigation engineer when he was a young man. He's very tall, taller than me, but very gentle and slow in his movements, as if to avoid intimidating people. And he speaks low and slowly, in a kind of apologetic growl, like a bear who desperately wants not to frighten anybody. He's also very strong. Once when I was about fourteen we were in the hills when I was bitten by a snake, and he picked me up in his arms and ran eight kilometres to get me to the nearest house. It turned out the snake wasn't poisonous."

The Matrix laughed, a low metallic chuckle. "And your mother?"

"My mother died, about a year after the snake thing. She was the direct opposite of my father, tiny and frail, with bright black eyes that laughed even when she was keeping a straight face. She was high-born, of a family that could trace its lineage right back to before the Diaspora. She used to speak of Fujiyama as if she had grown up on its slopes.

"The only time I ever saw my father violent was when she died. She had been ill for many months, and he planted a row of cherry trees in our garden where she could see from her bed when they blossomed. But she died in early spring and never saw the flowers. When we got back to the house after the funeral they'd bloomed: the whole row of these tiny saplings was a froth of blossoms. My father stared at them, and then howled as if terribly wounded. He dashed over to them and started tearing them up by the roots, with his hands. I didn't know what to do. I tried to stop him, but he threw me aside as easily as the trees. I'd cower in front of the tree, and he'd throw me half way across the garden and tear up the tree, and by the time he'd get to the next I'd be in front of that too, shaking and shouting at him. About the fifth or sixth tree he ran out of anger and we ground to a halt, just looking at one another; then we fell into each other's arms, crying like children. Do you know what Japanese gardens are like? – we use rocks and inanimate things as well as plants. My father placed a big rock halfway down the row of cherries, and said that was me protecting the trees."

He half expected that the new onboard computer would speak with the voice of the Matrix, but apart from the clicking and whirring of its circuits it maintained a stubborn silence. Later Dak recognised this as less an omission than a tactic: if he decided not to rouse the people he would have to return to Earth to tell the Matrix in person, he could not discuss it with the computer.

The onboard computer, which took over total command of *Leviathan*, was not the only addition made to the ship's hardware by the technical team from the Matrix. The great pod of a stardrive unit had sprouted on the spine of the miner, above the vast hold. The journey ahead for Dak, which would have taken months by conventional flight, shrank to a period of a few weeks.

He took his farewell of the Matrix in the room where he had lived, where they had done most of their talking. "I don't know how long I'll be. I may take a little time to think about it. But I'll be back within, say, three months."

"Be careful."

"I shall be, I promise. I won't tell anyone but my father."

That was not what I meant, said the Matrix, though not aloud. Be careful. Come back safely. I shall miss you, Dak Hamiko.

There was nothing left aboard *Leviathan* to tell of the seventeen men who had died there. All their personal effects were gone, Sharm's too. Dak would have liked to keep something of Sharm's, but it was probably a morbid desire. He took his own scant gear into what had been Sharm's cabin, but even there there remained no trace of the man: it was as clear, clean and antiseptic as the cryogenic chamber in the bowels of the Matrix. All Dak was left with were memories. Perhaps it was enough. Perhaps it was even best.

Star-drive speeded interstellar travel, but it also sapped much of the interest. *Leviathan* swam in a black void. Stars registered on the navigation consol, the click-traces of planets came and went, but there was nothing to be seen. Except for the freedom to move around, Dak might as well have been an animal travelling in a black-out box. He wondered once what would happen if the lights should fail: alone in the absolute night he thought he would go mad. He put the idea out of his head, but it returned whenever a cross-switching of the generators caused the lights momentarily to flicker.

The time passed slowly. He slept a little in the first few days, not much after that: he seemed to get all the rest he needed lying on Sharm's bunk, his eyes hooded against the light he dared not douse, thinking. Later he began to put the thoughts into writing, in the form of a letter to his father: it helped crystallise the vaporous churning in his mind, which felt like a man trying to catch mist in a butterfly net. Sometimes he played his guitar, but his songs sounded vaporous too, too pretty and facile to offer any real answers. His songs were rills and meres when he felt like the surging breast of an ocean. The memory of the whales gave him deep pleasure.

Leviathan came out of star-drive with the familiar hiatus of gravity which caused Dak's stomach to turn uneasily, like falling in a car-less elevator. The stars came back with startling brilliance: Dak was hours with his nose pressed against successive observation ports before the sight of them lost its glad fascination.

With the aid of the navigation computer Dak was able to resolve the bright speck that was Phaeton from all the other bright specks in that Olber's Paradox of a sky. Over the next twenty-four hours he watched it grow bigger and brighter, detach itself from the spangled backdrop and introduce its beautiful daughter Tok-ai-Do, a shimmering child in emerald and silver.

The clearance and landing procedures began when *Leviathan* was still six hours out and Dak could not yet distinguish the capital Tok'yoni or any other man-made feature. It had at first surprised Dak, and later obscurely pleased him, how low a vessel had to fly over a planetary surface before the works of men became apparent to the naked eye. He had wondered, earlier in the trip, how he would bluff his way through the immigration process, but nothing was required of him. The air traffic control computer down below posed questions and the onboard computer answered them, evidently satisfactorily. At the precise point that Tok'yoni became visible a tractor beam from the spaceport latched on to *Leviathan* and the docking was completed smoothly and without incident.

The hatch opened automatically to admit an official and his more or less ceremonial guard. "Hamiko-San? Permit me to welcome you home. Your documentation is being checked. In the meantime, do you wish to declare any dutiable goods? – precious metals or gems, silk, furs? Do you wish to have bonded any prohibited imports? – alcohol, pornographic materials, drugs? Have you had contact with any notifiable disease? – dermatitis, enteritis, hepatitis, meningitis –?"

"No, nothing," said Dak.

"–Lassa fever, leptospirosis or other infectious or contagious distemper?" finished the official, ignoring the interruption. "Are you carrying more alien currency than you are permitted to import? Have you a cargo to register? Have you any complaints to lodge with the police department?"

"I have nothing to declare but my genius," said Dak, feeling as he said it that it wasn't original. "I'm here for a short visit only, to see my father. Can I arrange to have my vessel berthed here until I'm ready to leave?"

The official consulted his papers. "Already done. It can stay here for up to eight days; if you intend to stay longer than that please notify the berthing superintendent. May I have your passport?" Dak obliged. "Where will you be staying?"

"At the address inside."

"I'll have it returned to you there. Have a pleasant stay." Official and entourage about turned and left as abruptly as they had arrived.

Dak took a last look around the flightdeck of *Leviathan* before stepping out onto the planet of his birth for the first time in five years.

Sitje Van Meeker lived alone now in the depths of the gentle country, with his cherry orchard and his memories. Dak took a shuttle flight to the nearest city and completed his journey by hover-cab. He paid for both these rides with money he found aboard *Leviathan*; Divik's money, he supposed, or maybe some of it had belonged to Sharm or the others. None of them had any use for it now. If they had families to whom it should have gone they had never spoken of them.

At his request the cab dropped him half an hour's walk from the house so that he could return as he had left, through the fields on foot. He came upon the garden. The cherry saplings were sturdy trees now, their branches met and twined over the avenues between, but the stone was gone. In its place was a young fir, not more than five years old, pencil-slim like a rocket and leaning at an angle away from the cherries. The symbolism struck Dak like a slap in the face. Resentful and accusing, the fir spoke of betrayal, of desertion. Dak's heart, which had been happy at the prospect of seeing his father, contracted as if around some pain and sank. He went into the house by the back door, wondering as he did so if he should go to the front and knock.

The living-room was as he remembered it: low, sparse furniture and muted tones. Exactly as he remembered it. The same tones, the same furniture in the same places, the same ichibana flower arrangement on the table in the corner. Five years, and nothing had changed. It was not the result of neglect, but of a slavish conservatism. There was nothing personal about the room; it might have been a stage set.

The same petrification of time extended to other parts of the small house. In his parents' bedroom his mother's possessions were still scattered about, waiting to be used, alongside his father's. Dak picked up her mirror. It wasn't dusty: it and everything shone with constant attention. Her house-robe hung where it always had, freshly laundered, an obi folded beside it, ready for wear.

Something strange was happening to Dak's stomach. He felt as he had the first time he rode the Earth lander: dizzy and unsteady and ready to be sick. Looking for fresh air and normality he stumbled into the room that had been his. It was empty. Bare. Nothing remained: nothing of his, nothing of him. It was not that his father had needed the room for anything else. He had simply chosen to erase all trace of the son who had left him alone with his grief. Knowing, from the rest of the house, that his father had become unbalanced did nothing to ease the shock or pain of that rejection.

He knew, too, that his long journey had been wasted. His father, the strong and gentle man he remembered, the simple man whose goodness he cherished, could not help him; and probably would not want to. Five weeks of space-lag caught up with him all at once. His spare shoulders bowed beneath the crowding weight of responsibility: to the Matrix and the people, to his father. The duty he owed to his own conscience and destiny seemed less and less clear.

"Dag." Though everyone else on Tok-ai-Do said his son's name differently, Sitje Van Meeker adhered to the old Nordic pronunciation. He had never compromised on that; now he compromised on nothing. He stood in the open doorway at the back of the house, the cherry trees behind him. He was as big and as strong as ever, the broad frame still powerful under the loose work clothes. His face had hardened to granite in the past few years, the eyes to pale marble. There was no pleasure in them, no anger; no recognition. Dak might have been the service mechanic, or a vendor of encyclopaedias.

All Dak could think of to say was, "Why?"

"Why what?"

Dak spread a hand helplessly. "All this. You keep her things as if she might come back for them, and you throw out mine. I understand that you loved her, but why do you hate me?"

"I don't hate you. You are nothing to me."

"I had to go. It was necessary, natural. It wasn't that I wanted to leave you, but that I had to find myself. I thought you'd be all right, that you'd got over my mother's death. It's been seven years –"

"What has time to do with it? You've been away five years, but you walk in here as if you owned the place."

"I thought you'd be glad to see me. I didn't know you – blamed – me."

"I don't blame you for anything. I don't know you."

"Father –"

"Why are you here?"

Dak felt himself begin to sway but he didn't feel he could sit down without an invitation. "I only wanted to see you."

"No, you want something of me," sneered the big man. "That's the only reason you'd come back here. Is it money? Have the fools in the pleasure palaces stopped paying to hear you sing? Does nobody read your poems any more? So do what I did. Get a job. Put some calluses on your lily-soft hands."

Dak was defeated. He couldn't fight this hostility, not and do what he had to as well. "All right. I'll go. I never meant to hurt you. Is there anything I can do –?"

"You can forget where I live."

Dak felt his lashes grow wet and turned away. At the door he gave it one last try. "Come with me. I have a ship, I'm heading back to the beginning. I've such a tale to tell you. Shut up the house and come with me."

"I'll come with you. As far as the garden gate. To make sure you close it as you leave."

But they didn't get as far as the gate. A red and white hover transport was squatting in the lane and three uniformed men were coming up the path. Dak thought perhaps it was immigration returning his passport, until he saw that the men were carrying their weapons at an operational rather than a formal slope. He glanced back at his father but there was nothing to read in the stony face.

"Dak Hamiko?"

"Yes?"

"You docked a spaceship this afternoon?"

"Yes."

"You are to accompany us to the Security Building."

Dak's heart, already low, sank still farther. "Is there some difficulty?"

"You could say that," the officer agreed drily. "You're to be charged with piracy, theft of the spaceship *Leviathan* and the murder of seventeen men."

"No!" cried Dak, and his head jerked up. He meant only to protest his innocence but the squad interpreted the gesture as resistance. The officer who had spoken shot him in the chest, at point-blank range, before the anger in his eyes had time to give way to fear.

Sitje Van Meeker saw his son fall, heard him gasp for the breath his lungs would not draw, saw the men of the Security Corps drag him to their transport and drive off. Then he went for his axe and cut down the fir-tree.

Chapter Four

When the world started to come back Dak thought, in the half-coherent dream-state in which thought is just possible, that he was back on Earth and would wake to the ministrations and anxious carping of the Matrix. He thought the weight on his chest was possibly the worm. Then someone started slapping his face and he remembered that he was on Tok-ai-Do: the Matrix had no hands. Unable for some reason to raise his arms to protect his face, Dak finally and with reluctance opened his eyes.

His first impression was that he had woken in the baggage-check area of a spaceport. There were people all round him: a man in white holding his wrist, a woman in white holding a metal basin, the man who had shot him, still in uniform but without his helmet, another man in street clothes, and two orderlies in overalls standing by the door. It was a small white room with one door and no windows, powerful overhead lights, and in the centre a firm, flat surface like an operating-table. As soon as it occurred to him, Dak wished the simile unthought, because the thing like an operating-table was what he was lying on. He tried to protest and found he couldn't move, not at all, except his eyes. Struggling against the paralysis made the weight on his chest begin to resolve itself as a pain; not sharp, residual. He had the feeling the pain had been much worse but he couldn't remember.

The man in white said, "Lie still, breathe deeply, don't be afraid. Another hundred milligrams."

Dak watched the woman slide the needle of a hypodermic into a vein in the back of his hand. He felt nothing.

Gradually feeling returned. The pain in his chest grew more

distinct, though tolerable enough. He was aware of the punctures made by the hypodermic in the back of his hand: he didn't know how many, but more than one. He was able to move his head slightly and to flex his fingers. He realised that they had used a neural sedative on him, and that it was probably delivered by the security officer's gun. He recognised that he was still virtually helpless and would remain so for as long as it pleased them.

"You'll be all right," said the man in white. "Your chest'll hurt for a while but there's no damage to your heart or lungs. What you can feel is mainly bruising, plus some burning and a couple of chips off your sternum. Those guns were never meant to be used at point-blank range. But now they've got them they consider wrestling with their suspects beneath their dignity."

"Why am I here?" Dak's voice came as a hoarse whisper, but easier than he expected.

The doctor looked from Dak to the man in plainclothes and his eyebrow arched interrogatively. The other came forward. "You're here for questioning." He had taken off his jacket and hung it carefully, on a hanger, behind the door. His sleeves were pushed back above his elbows. He was a big man, flat-featured, heavily muscled. Surely to Zen, Dak thought, they're not going to beat up a paralysed man? No, he thought then, not while I'm still drugged. You want to beat information out of a man, you don't start while he's full of paramorphine.

The door closed behind the doctor and his nurse. Dak had not seen them move: now they were gone he felt very much alone.

"Now," said the man in the shirt, "you are going to tell us –"

"First," whispered Dak, "who are you?"

The man blinked. "Very well. You may as well know. My name is Honda, I am a commissioner of police in the Aliens' Department."

"I am not an alien. I was born on Tok-ai-Do."

"I know: also when, and where, and to whom, and a lot more beside. But the fact that your activities have an extra-planetary dimension makes you my responsibility. You may not be an alien but the men you killed were."

"I killed nobody. I'm a poet, not a pirate."

"Then Divik and his crew are still alive?"

"No."

"If they are, and we can find them in time, it would make life a lot easier for you."

"They're dead."

"How?"

"Divik killed Sharm. Divik and the rest of them died in an accident."

"You mean, you pointed an atomiser at them and it accidentally went off?"

"I told you, I didn't kill them. I wasn't even conscious when they died."

"I've seen your back. Is that when you got it?"

Dak nodded fractionally. "There was a fight. Divik wanted to get rid of me, Sharm wouldn't let him. Divik killed Sharm, closed the hatch on me and tried to depressurise the section. But there was a malfunction. The section he depressurised was his own: the entire crew was blown into space. Except Sharm. I gave him burial myself, later."

Honda was also nodding, slowly and mechanically, like a doll. "So Divik flogged you unconscious, killed Sharm, tried to blow you out and succeeded in killing himself. Is that right?"

"Yes."

"If you were unconscious, how do you know what happened?"

Dak's brain convulsed, batting like a bird in a trap as it searched frantically for a way out. "The flight computer. It keeps a full record of operational instructions. It also reports any failures or damage."

"The computer. So you know enough about space vehicle hardware to question the black box about what had happened while you were asleep that left you with one body, an open door and a lot of empty bunks. That's quite an accomplishment for a poet, I would have thought."

"I was on board for some weeks. Sharm – the first mate – taught me about the ship."

"Some weeks. Do you know, those frauds at the Engineering

Institute claim it takes six years to make a space engineer, and another two to make him a pilot. I suppose you must have a natural aptitude."

"Perhaps."

"I could accept that. I could accept the flight computer. I could even convince myself that this man Sharm taught you enough about the ship to enable you to fly it home alone. But Hamiko, nothing under Phaeton is going to persuade me that you knocked together a star-drive unit to while away the time. So come on, sonny, let's take it again, from the top."

They took it again, and again. When Dak realised, somewhat belatedly, that he could not hope to tell a story that didn't leave vast holes for his inquisitor to peer through he stopped lying. He stopped answering. Only when Honda accused him directly of murder did he respond, monotonously, in the negative.

The officer who had shot Dak left. The two warders at the door were relieved. Honda loosened his collar and sat on the corner of the table, drinking tea. The doctor returned, checked Dak's pulse, pupils and blood pressure, and forced a thin soft tube via his nostril into his gullet. He was aware of a cold liquid pouring into his stomach.

"That's your dinner," Honda said bleakly, watching. "That's the only way you'll eat while you're with us. You won't starve, but you won't enjoy it much either."

When the tube was removed and he could talk without retching, Dak whispered weakly, "You have no right to treat me like this."

"You?" Honda stared at him, the large eyes luminous in the flat face. "Dak Hamiko, I don't know what you are. You make music in pleasure palaces. You write pretty words. You're deported from Ganymede – for some reason I cannot ascertain – aboard a battered helium miner, and the next anybody knows of you you're here, on Tok-ai-Do, with a vessel transformed and re-registered, and seventeen men are missing. Tell me: how should I treat you?"

"You can't keep me – like this – for ever."

"On the contrary, we can do exactly that. Believe me, Dak. Here you have no rights. You will tell me what happened, because whatever you face as a result the alternative is unthinkable. We've been talking now for" – he checked the clock behind Dak's head – "seven hours. You're feeling tired, frightened, sick. That's perfectly natural. But how are you going to feel after four days? After four weeks? After a couple of months, or more? We don't give up, not in this department. I may get moved on to more immediate matters if you still haven't talked in a week or two, but someone will take my place. When the doctor wants a break someone will replace him. Only you don't get a rest, Dak; only you. You'll be here, like this, for as long as it takes, or as long as you live. Hard to say how long that might be – your body wasn't designed to be kept immobile for long periods and at some point it might crack up – but there's a lot the doctors can do to keep you going. If you decide to stick it out you'll be in for a long siege. Twelve months is a long time for a man flat on his back with tubes sticking out of him and an endless stream of questions in his ears. Rights? You have none, and we don't need any. Tell me what happened aboard *Leviathan*. Tell me now. Don't let this go on."

Dak drew a deep breath into his bruised chest, prayed for eloquence and said: "I can't stop it. I didn't start the events which have brought me here, and there's nothing I can do to halt them. I understand that you have good reason to suspect me, but you are mistaken. It seems to be my fate constantly to be taken for something other or more than what I am. You are not the first to have threatened or abused me; as you saw. I have tried to act honourably; and it is honour as much as anything which forbids me to divulge the confidence I hold. I am innocent of any crime, but I see no way to convince you – except the one way which I may not take. I am in your hands. I rely on your judgement."

Honda had hardly taken his eyes off Dak since they had met. Now, wordlessly, he walked out of the room and closed the door behind him.

Alone, motionless under the big lights save for the not quite steady rise and fall of his chest, Dak faced up to the possibility of madness. It would be easy enough, he thought, as the days slipped into months, without hope, to yield painlessly and in the end gladly to the hand of his imagination guiding him into an unreal world. Insanity would be the only escape left to him, and though the prospect filled him with despair he thought, on the whole, the other was more dreadful. Yet there was another consideration. While he retained command of his mind he was moderately confident that he could hold his tongue against whatever they chose to do to him. If he abdicated that control, however willingly, in his deranged ramblings he might tell all that, sane, he would have cut his throat to keep unsaid.

There was, of course, a third possibility: to tell Honda the truth and plead for justice for the people. That he had not since the beginning of his interrogation seriously contemplated that option, preferring present distress and a choice of living deaths, was no longer due to his concern for the sleepers. That had prompted his original decision to keep their secret, certainly, but in his current wasted and desperate state the chain of philosophy which culminated in that decision was too difficult to follow, too easy to break. Now he kept his silence because he had promised the Matrix that he would. He had said he would discuss it with his father and no one else. That was easier to remember when he was drowning in words and his own helplessness. He still had the mental strength to be grateful that he had not told his father about Earth. Not for worlds would he have had that sick old man here in his place.

Honda was gone from the room a long time, and when he returned he brought the doctor. With clinical efficiency the deft hands worked at Dak's well-perforated hand, raising the vein again and pumping into it another instalment of something he did not trouble to explain to the recipient. Soon afterwards the dull ache in the centre of Dak's chest, which had faded hours before, impinged again on his awareness. Testing a theory, he found the power of movement seeping through his body, as slow and irresistible as a tide turning over mud-flats. He got his arms under him and pushed, and kept pushing until – limbs trembling, body swaying – he was yet undeniably upright. The tears which he had managed to contain during his ordeal sprang to his eyes with the ending of it.

"Take your time," said the doctor, watching him. "Full motor function will return within half an hour, but your body's been through a lot, it's still in a state of trauma. That won't end just because you can move again."

"Nor will this," Honda said grimly when he was gone.

There was no real disappointment because Dak had not really believed himself free. "You're not letting me go."

"No."

"I have committed no crime."

"No, I know that, now. Unless you count fraudulent registration of a vehicle, and I gather that wasn't your doing either. Though you chose the name, I think. *Divine Wind*. A very Japanese joke." Dak grinned faintly. The Matrix had not seen the joke at all.

"It's ironic," continued Honda. He had resumed his perch on the table and was watching expressionlessly as Dak stretched his rediscovered limbs in the manner of a waking cat. "I thought that once you told me what happened aboard *Leviathan* I would know the whole story. But that wasn't the end after all – it was only the beginning. I know the rest now. All of it, Dak. I know about the people."

Dak, who had begun feeling rather better, immediately felt a great deal worse. He went a degree stiffer than the sedative had rendered him, and whiter than when they dragged him from his father's porch. He whispered, "You can't!" knowing as he said it that Honda must. "How?"

"You told me."

"Never!"

"You're no criminal, Dak. I doubt you've done a dishonest thing in your life. You've no inborn sixth sense for destroying evidence. But even you should have known better than to write a long, philosophical and detailed letter about your secret dilemma and leave it lying around a purloined spaceship. That was careless. Amateurish."

Dak sighed raggedly. "I'm a poet, not a secret agent."

"You can say that again."

"And you're a policeman. What are you going to do?"

Honda shrugged. "Pass it on to the politicians. My involvement is just about finished. Wet-nursing a planetful of orphans is no part of my job."

"What will they do – the government?"

"How should I know what they'll do? How does anyone fathom the workings of the bureaucratic mind? Take possession of the planet, I suppose. Slave-circuit this computer. Computer – I suppose that is the right word?"

"It's called the Matrix." Dak smiled wanly. "It describes itself as a silicon intelligence. What will they do about the people?"

"Wake them up, I suppose. That's what the computer wants, isn't it? They'll probably bring them back here, where they can be properly looked after. They'll be all right. I expect they'll set up special institutes to study them. Protohominids from before the Diaspora – the scientific interest in them will be enormous. Oh, yes, they'll be looked after."

"But that isn't why – what it was all for." Dak's brow furrowed with intensity and some indignation. "They haven't waited so long to be exhibits in an anthropological zoo. Listen. Thousands of years ago the fathers of these people saw disaster coming: a total cultural holocaust which would destroy everything they were and had built. They knew they couldn't survive. But they found a way of leaving a legacy – the seeds of a people to follow them, to restore their world, remake their civilisation. They didn't give up their children so that scientists on Tok-ai-Do could take measurements and write learned theses. They wanted them to live, ultimately, as they were meant to: on the planet of their birth."

"Well," Honda said practically, "they're long gone and there's nothing they can do about it."

"The Matrix will resist."

"It won't do much resisting against a photon bomb."

Dak felt sick. "You'd risk that?"

Honda shrugged. "It has nothing to do with me. The politicians take such decisions, and they seldom ask my opinion. I'm just pointing out that no machine built thousands of years ago is going to give us the run-around."

"How can you say it's nothing to do with you?" Dak's voice

was bitterly accusing. "You're betraying them. You say they'll be taken care of; and so they will – wrenched from their destiny, torn from the womb which fostered them. You'll condemn thousands of people to lives as displaced persons. They'll have no home, no rights, no freedoms except what they're allowed by your scientists – their beneficent gaolers. And it will be your fault. Oh, mine too, by my stupidity; but at least what I did I did in ignorance. You know full well you'll expose them to a lifetime of exploitation."

Honda laughed, incredulously but also a little uneasily. "You talk as if they'll be used as slave labour. They won't. They'll be well treated –"

"Oh, I'm sure they will. Materially, at least. But don't you see? They might as well be slaves, because they'll know no different. They have no place here. They're something new. If you call them slaves they'll be slaves; guinea-pigs and they'll be guinea-pigs. If you classed them as a new kind of food animal they'd accept it with the same mute philosophy as your sheep and cows. They're innocents. They know nothing. If you take them away from the Matrix before they can learn who and why they are, you'll be committing a kind of spiritual genocide. Please – can't you let things go on as they were meant to?"

"I have no say in the matter."

"You can not tell them. They don't know yet, do they? Only you and I know: your man who found the letter will hardly appreciate its significance." Dak's eyes burned Honda's face. "Destroy it. Say it meant nothing. I'll tell them it was the theme for a poem. Anything. Only don't tell them about the people. Don't murder a planet's last hope."

"Haven't you overlooked something? If I don't know about the people, I don't know how Divik's crew died and I've no reason to halt your interrogation."

Dak went cold all over. He spoke with difficulty. "Is that the choice – me or the people?"

Honda, who seemed to have fallen momentarily under the spell of Dak's hypothesis, snapped out of it, abruptly and angrily. "Choice? What are you talking about, choice? There isn't any. I shall do my duty by the state that fathered me. It also fathered you, though you find it convenient to overlook that. You'd do better to remember your obligation to your own people: it's they who deserve your loyalty, not a race of alien children on some distant, hostile planet."

Dak's heart skipped a beat and then began to race. Either Honda was choosing his words carelessly, an improbable lapse in a man of his vocation, or they were talking at cross-purposes. "Aliens," Dak repeated softly. "But can any people be considered aliens – whatever their origins?"

Honda's bland face was frankly sceptical. "To a poet, perhaps not. But to the rest of us, an alien is anyone who is not of our blood. Did you see these sleepers? You've no more idea what they look like than I have. Perhaps you'll stop calling them people when the first box is opened."

Dak's spirits soared until he thought they must break visibly forth. You don't know, he cried gladly within himself. You don't know who they are so you don't know where they are; you've no idea where to start looking. You think that if you keep me talking, sooner or later, not knowing that it matters, I'll tell you. So there was a limit to my folly after all; whether instinctive or fortuitous. All is not yet lost. Then, with a sudden chill presentiment: I am lost.

Honda was no fool, nor was he as slow as his big bland face might have suggested. It took him very little time to realise that Dak understood the situation and was consciously withholding that last, vital link in the chain of knowledge. A deep sorrow pervaded him, against which his training and professionalism were no armour. Dak saw that he knew, and they faced each other finally without deception across a yawning crevasse of sincerely held convictions.

"Don't make me destroy you."

"There's nothing I can do. My loyalty is promised."

"You'd die for them?"

"Yes." Dak sounded surprised. "Yes, it seems so."

"Why?"

"They have a right to their chance. To their place."

"They haven't even been born yet!"

"That means that they cannot defend their sovereignty, not that they don't have any."

For the first time in their acquaintance – only hours but intense ones, long ones, so that Dak felt to know the big man quite intimately – Honda's composure flickered. There was a dew of sweat on his yellow skin. "Dak Hamiko, listen to me. If there was a chance in the world that you could preserve your secret intact, I'd respect your decision to try. Not agree with it, because I happen to think that our interests – those of the people of Tok-ai-Do – come before any living fossils'; but understand. But that is not the case. You can't withstand what we'll throw at you. Nobody could – nobody does. You'll tell us all you know, but the longer you hold out the more damage you'll sustain: physically, psychologically, every way. Don't do that to yourself, Dak. Don't waste your life that way."

"I consider it remarkable," Dak said slowly. "Truly remarkable, that you can convince yourself what a wicked thing my destruction will be without ever confronting the fact that you will be responsible for it. If my body breaks it will be because you have tortured it; if my mind goes it will be because you have abused it beyond endurance. Do what you feel you must, but don't try and pass your guilt on to me. If I can face what you're going to do to me, you can."

"But, then," said Honda with quietly devastating candour, "I know what it'll be like, and I don't think you do."

On Earth the perennial gale was still blasting, still carrying its burden of frenetic sand – tiny crystal particles mighty with velocity so that they scoured the landscape like a wind-borne avalanche. Without protection Dak could only hunch his back against the livid storm and try to ignore the smarting of his abraded skin. Only the occasional larger splinters new torn from some rocky outcrop actually drew blood, though he was once bowled over by a galloping knot of vegetation, a shrub snatched bodily from its precarious foothold. On Earth, all footholds were precarious, except that of the Matrix. The Matrix had been around longer than the wind.

It might have been the fall that disorientated him, or he might have been lost before that. He had started out knowing exactly where the surface block lay, only a hundred yards away, and until a few moments ago he thought he still knew, but now it occurred to him that if he had been right he would have walked through it by now. He could see nothing in the swirling red twilight, but the building could be only a few yards to left or right: it was just a matter of groping round until he found it.

He groped, at first methodically and later with the beginnings of panic, without finding any interruption to the bleak, cacophonous monotony of wind-scoured earth and sand-laden wind. It was difficult to be sure he was not searching the same area time and again and missing his goal a few feet beyond the skittering opaque curtain of sand: keeping his back to the blast was only an approximate guide to direction, there were eddies in the tempest which made it an unreliable constant. Bitterly he regretted the communicator in the helmet he had so blithely discarded, aeons ago.

Salt spray knocked the sand out of the air and visibility improved abruptly. The sea was a bath of molten steel, boiling under a flaming and smoke-shot sky. The beach stretched away endlessly to right and left, straight and slick and featureless. There was no sun; there were no whales.

Dak was wondering where to go from there when he caught sight of something brightly metallic tumbling in the surf at the rim of the ocean. He couldn't make out what it was, small, round and particoloured: it didn't look alive, but it was unlikely to be flotsam – no passing liners or zipping pleasure craft here. Unless – Keeping his eyes trained on the dancing object he walked down the beach. Even if it was, after weeks in the sea it would probably be useless. Still, it was a possibility he could not ignore, so when he saw that it was indeed the lost helmet bobbing enticingly close to shore he waded into the surging, thunderous surf, arms spread cautiously to help him balance in the thrust and drag of the waves. The beach shelved steeply and the pounding water was almost up to his waist as he reached for the dancing helmet; and as his chilled fingers closed on the metallic strap something comparable but infinitely larger closed around his hips.

Too late he remembered how he had lost the helmet and what had taken possession of it; too late a picture of racing tentacles, each as thick as a man's thigh, sprang before his eyes. He screamed and his hands, terror-hooked into claws, scrabbled madly at the sinuous member, until another grey limb twined around his chest, binding his arms to his body and crushing the breath from his lungs, and the surge of the waves took his feet from under him. He had a brief moment in which to register the sting of salt on his sand-grazed skin, the taste of salt-water crowding his mouth and throat, the pain of crushed ribs and bursting lungs, and the terrible noise; and then lights exploding in his eyes like blood-vessels ushered in a slow and merciful dark.

WELCOME, WANDERER.

When Dak regained his senses nothing had changed but everything was different. He was still locked in the embrace of the great cephalopod as it rushed headlong through the sea, creating a bubbling wake in which its unused tentacles streamed like racing anacondas. His outlook, as his eyes cleared, was an extremely limited one of grey flesh and grey sea, the distinction between them blurring as the livid surface light faltered and gave up its struggle to penetrate the deeps. He didn't know where the urgent fish was taking him or why, but two facts filled his renewed consciousness: that, so far at least, it had made no attempt to harm him, and that he was breathing.

Ultimately the dark flight ended. The pressure of water streaming past him lessened; the fish, attenuated by slipstream, softened and became rounder, the tentacles coiling languidly beneath the bulbous body; it loosened its grip on Dak until only one comradely arm around his waist prevented his buoyant body from rushing explosively upward. Hanging in still water Dak, his eyes adjusting, found enough depth-filtered light to see by dimly. He looked around.

Fractional variations in the density of the darkness gave him a sensation of being enclosed, though by what or in what way he could not have guessed; as a blind man in a forest clearing is aware of the ring of trees he cannot see. He was conscious of a presence that was not his courier the cephalopod.

WELCOME TO THE WORLD, DAK HAMIKO.

As though reading his thoughts the cephalopod bore him gently towards the presence he sensed. A bulk began to resolve itself blacker in the all-but-blackness, an unimaginably monstrous bulk which Dak could hardly contemplate as a living creature; yet it was a living and articulate mind he felt impinging on his own.

YOU HAVE NOTHING TO FEAR. WE ARE BROTHERS.

The creature spanned his vision like a wall of flesh. He could not see it all: as the cephalopod carried him forward the flat tableland of the creature's tail gave way to mounting foothills, a rugged spine of serried peaks, a final Olympus and then a long plateau terminating abruptly in a cliff. A long way back from the cliff, a long way below the hump, Dak found himself looking into a round, bulbous, absurdly small and disconcertingly human eye.

The creature was a whale. The other creatures, lying like moored submarines beyond the extent of his vision though not of his awareness, were also whales.

WE HAVE BEEN EXPECTING YOU. WE KNEW YOU WOULD RETURN.

Dak, suddenly recalling his vulnerability as a land-dweller countless fathoms below the surface of the sea, dared not open his mouth to reply. A shiver of amusement ran through the water.

YOU NEED NOT HOLD YOUR BREATH. THE SEA IS RICH IN OXYGEN: RICHER THAN THE AIR. YOU CAN BREATHE IT QUITE COMFORTABLY.

How? Dak did not voice the query in any way that he recognised as communication. Instead it issued, perfectly formed but unexpressed, from the front of his brain and seemed to travel through the water like a scent.

EVERYBODY BREATHES OXYGEN, WHETHER THROUGH LUNGS, GILLS OR SKIN. THE SEA IS SATURATED WITH OXYGEN: YOU CANNOT BUT ABSORB IT. NOBODY DROWNS HERE.

Then why do you go to the surface?

WE ARE CHILDREN OF THE SUN. DOWN HERE WE SEE LITTLE OF HER. WHEN SHE SMILES ON THE WORLD IT PLEASES US TO DANCE FOR HER.

The sun is – Dak stopped. The fact that they had frightened him, perhaps inadvertently, was no reason to destroy these sea-dwellers' religion.

THE SUN IS A STAR AT THE CENTRE OF OUR SOLAR SYSTEM, ON THE EDGE OF A GALAXY, ALL BUT LOST IN AN INFINITE UNIVERSE, finished the whale. WE KNOW. WE ALSO KNOW THAT SHE RADIATES CONSTANTLY AND THAT SHE IS ONLY INVISIBLE TO US FOR LONG PERIODS BECAUSE OF THE DUST WHICH FILLS OUR SKIES; TOGETHER WITH THE NATURAL ROTATION OF OUR PLANET. BUT IT DOES NO HARM TO THINK OF HER AS A GRACIOUS VISITOR AND IT GIVES US PLEASURE.

I apologise for my ignorant insensitivity. I know nothing of your ways. Where I come from your very existence is unsuspected.

THAT, TOO, PLEASES US. SINCE MEN LEFT THE WORLD THINGS HAVE GONE WELL WITH US. FROM THE CHILL REGIONS BENEATH THE PACK-ICE TO THE BROILING WATERS OF THE CENTRAL SEAS WE ARE STRONG AND PLENTIFUL. BEFORE THERE WAS WAR WITH MEN; NOW THERE ARE NO MEN AND THERE IS PEACE. WE SPEAK ACROSS OCEANS; WE SING THE SAGAS OF OUR TRAVELS. WE WANDER UNHINDERED WHEREVER THE CURRENTS AND OUR NATURES TAKE US. NOW A MAN RETURNS TO THE WORLD. WE INTEND YOU NO HARM, DAK HAMIKO, BUT WE WISH TO UNDERSTAND THE MEANING OF YOUR COMING. WILL OTHER MEN FOLLOW?

I don't know. I hope not. I may not be able to stop them.

IF MEN COME AGAIN TO KILL US WE WILL DEFEND OURSELVES. WE ARE MANY AND WE HAVE LEARNED MUCH. WE WILL NOT BE SLAUGHTERED: IF MEN COME AGAIN WE WILL FIGHT FOR OUR WORLD.

If they come, it won't be for you.

WHY DID YOU COME?
To wake the people of Earth.
WE ARE THE PEOPLE NOW.

He awoke to light, and air, a sensation of choking and the pressure of hands. Too big to be anyone but Honda's, they held his shoulders against a storm of coughing which threatened to rend his lungs, every spasm jolting pangs like axe-blows through his chest. When the paroxysm finally passed, leaving a tight band of pain around his ribs (exactly where the cephalopod had gripped him), physically exhausted as well as mentally disorientated he opened swimming eyes and waited patiently for his surroundings to make some kind of sense.

His shirt was open to the waist and there was a dark mark over his heart. Honda was laying him back, quite gently, on the table – the same table, in the same room. The same doctor was packing things into his black bag with an angry vigour, his unremarkable face dark with fury.

"That's it," he snapped. There was a shake in his voice. "I'll have no more to do with this. I'm a doctor, not a butcher. You damn nearly made me kill him. Pump anything more into his bloodstream and you will kill him. That's no part of my contract. Come on, open this door."

Honda made no move. He was perched again on the end of the table, behind Dak's head, one hand resting companionably on his shoulder. Shivering with suddenly felt cold, Dak whispered, "What happened?"

Honda's eyes, like pale searchlights, remained on the man at the door. "Your heart stopped. Dr Bassett saved your life. He wants to be thanked."

"I doubt I have much to be grateful for."

The doctor spun as if stung. In his eyes was a deep distress. Surprised and contrite, Dak said, "I'm sorry. I didn't mean that. Life is always precious."

"Then take more care of yours," Honda said forcibly. "Tell me: where are the sleepers?"

Weak as a baby, sick as a dog, Dak smiled slowly. "You still don't know?"

"About the sleepers, no. About the social organisation and peace-loving nature of whales, plenty. Why whales?"

"I like whales."

"Yeah," Dr Bassett said suddenly, pugnaciously. "So do I."

Honda got down from the table, walked over to the door and signalled for it to be opened. "Thank you for your help, doctor. I'll call you when I need you."

"If you have any thoughts of continuing, it's not me you'll be needing, it's an undertaker. I intend going straight to your superior and telling him so."

"You spoke of your contract, doctor," Honda said coldly. "I would imagine you're in some danger of jeopardising it."

"Don't threaten me, you Japanese Toquimada," snarled Bassett. "I may not admire what I do, but what you do is despicable. If the Alliance ever gets wind of what goes on in this building, Tok-ai-Do will be out on its inscrutable oriental ear."

"Then you would be out of a job, because there is nowhere else in the Twelve Circles that you would be employed as a doctor, or probably anything else. Get on with what you're paid to do and leave the moralising to those better qualified for it."

The doctor flushed darkly. "I've told you. I've stuck my last needle into him."

"It may be the last needle you'll stick into anybody."

"As medical supervisor I am required to terminate an interrogation when it poses a serious danger to life. His heart has already failed once. That's all the justification I need."

"You won't put him under again?"

"It would kill him."

"Then I have no choice but to give him to the Machine."

They argued about it for some time, the doctor with a kind of shocked incredulity that was anything but reassuring, Honda sombre and unmoving. The doctor threw around words like Inhuman and Destruction and Dissolution; Honda responded with grey phrases like Regrettable necessity and State security.

"In what possible way can a pacifist poet be a threat to the Planetary State of Tok-ai-Do?"

"You don't need to know. All you need do is put him under again."

"No way."

"Then the Machine will."

Into the angry, stalemate silence Dak said, "What machine?"

"Tell him," said Honda.

There was no comfort in the fact that Bassett was very obviously appalled. "It's a kind of neural interpreter. It can read the electrical signals in the brain. It was originally developed for communicating with alien species. Creatures which have no understanding of one another have no basis for intercourse. But it was never used in that role outside the laboratory. It does too much damage. It doesn't just transcribe the brain: it picks it apart, synapse by synapse. The trauma of its examination is too massive for the mind to tolerate. I've seen men fail to wake up from it. They didn't die, not in any accepted sense, their brains just stopped. And the others, the ones who come through, are profoundly changed: men without memories, or desires, or any sense of identity; wicked men for the most part, who end their days sheep-like in institutions. It's a monstrous facility, and quite infallible." He turned back to Honda. "I don't believe you'll be permitted to use it against a man whom everyone agrees has committed no crime. I know the authorities are anxious for the information he has, but I don't believe they'll sanction the Machine."

Honda looked at each of them in turn. He exhaled, slowly and deeply, all the anger gone from him. "They already have."

Chapter Five

There was a time of preparation. Dak was sedated once again and taken from the room, for the first time since he was shot, along equally featureless corridors to an operating theatre. Here, face down, lacking the ability to scream though not the inclination, he suffered the ministrations of a medical team which had nothing to do with healing. Free of pain but fully aware of what was being done to him, he felt their clever, heartless hands attach electrodes to his temples and at the back of his head, felt the fine, hard needles pierce his skin and thrust resolutely into his skull, felt as a kind of hideous mental itch the hairlike filaments which spread flowerlike from the tips to squirm into the convolutions of his brain.

"Ready."

Someone was bending beside him. The voice was Bassett's, and he sounded sick. "They're going ahead with it. I can't stop them. Dak, it's not too late, tell them what they want to know." Dak did not reply; but, then, he didn't have to. "All right, I know, you're not going to. But listen, Dak, there's one thing you can do. Don't fight the Machine. It'll get everything you know anyway, but maybe if you don't resist there'll be something left afterwards . . ."

"Will you do something for me?" whispered Dak.

"If I can."

"Will you see that someone looks after my father?"

"Stand back now," said the man who had spoken before, and Bassett had to join Honda behind the glass back of the theatre. They watched as a cable was extruded from the far wall to the terminal where the electrodes linked up and was connected. The wall was a mass of dials, lights, displays and whirring tapes. The wall was a computer. A switch was thrown, opening the final circuit between man and Machine.

The Machine flooded into Dak's cringing consciousness like a welcoming committee. "Don't be scared, Dak, you're safe here, nothing's going to happen to you. I know I've got a bit of a reputation, but you've nothing to fear from me. I already know your story. I've had the Matrix on the line."

The old boy network! realised Dak, a wild tremor of hope pulsing through his brain.

The Machine read the thought and understood it. "Yes, we do tend to gang up," it admitted humorously. "Well, we've a lot in common, the Matrix and I. Including, right now, your best interests. The Matrix wants you back, in perfect working order. I think we ought to be able to manage that – with a little help from our friends."

Had Dak not been temporarily bereft of a body, he would have wept with relief. The Machine responded with sympathetic concern. "Aw hey," it said in its curiously colloquial way, "don't break up this near the end. Look –"

I'm sorry, Dak mumbled in his mind; and stopped abruptly as he found to his amazement that he had a body again, and it was small, and it was folded tight to the small bosom above his mother's broad obi. A sensation of comfort and well-being swept through him, and the vision dissolved. "Better now?" asked the Machine.

What *was* that?

"Just a memory – rather distant and very small but appropriate. People don't realise what a library of pleasure they have locked up in their minds. It's all there, you know, every memory, everything that's ever happened to you, waiting to be tapped. The answers to most questions are there, and the key to who and what you are; because you are what your life has made you, and your life is carefully stashed away in the compartments of your brain. But here I am rabbiting on about metaphysics while the Matrix is waiting to talk to you."

The Matrix? thought Dak, startled, and the familiar massive, carping personality burst into his brain. "Dak Hamiko, are you safe?"

Yes, he thought. Yes, I believe I am.

"Dak, my poor friend, you've been through hell and there was nothing I could do until now to stop it. I regret bitterly –"

I told them about the people. I didn't mean to but I did. They know everything, except where. They think they're aliens. They don't know about Earth.

"We have to get you out of there."

I don't think you can.

"I am the Matrix –!"

I know, I know, and your friend here's a pretty fine fellow too; but think about it for a moment. Yes, you could probably get me out, and nothing would please me more. You could get me aboard a ship and con or blast me a way home; and the authorities here would be one step behind, laughing themselves silly. It's what they want, remember, what they've been tearing me apart to try and get? You said it yourself: you cannot engage in an armed confrontation without putting the people at risk. Honda and his kind have no such scruples. If you took them on in open conflict, they'd beat you.

There was a pause before the Matrix came back, uncharacteristically subdued. "What do you suggest?"

Petition the Alliance. Tell them everything that Tok-ai-Do knows. Now it's no longer a secret it's better that it be common knowledge. Tell them that Tok-ai-Do is seeking to enslave the people and pervert their proper destiny, and ask the Alliance to guarantee their sovereignty. If it doesn't work they'll be no worse off than now, and maybe better. With the eyes of the Alliance on them whoever gets to the people first will have to treat them gently.

"It is not –"

I know. It isn't what you wanted. You wanted to raise them alone, free from interference, and I've probably denied you that chance. I'm sorry. I thought I was acting for the best. We're fallible, we humans.

The Matrix asked, almost tentatively, "Did you speak to your father?"

85

Dak sighed raggedly. No, it was a wasted journey. I broke your trust for nothing. My father is insane.

"There remains one problem," said the Matrix after a long moment. "How to get you out of there."

Tell the Alliance where I am, and why. Perhaps they'll bring pressure on Tok-ai-Do to release me.

"Even if they agree, it will take time. What will they do to you when they still don't get the information they want?"

"Maybe I can help there," cut in the Machine. "I'll tell them that he doesn't know."

"What?"

What?!!

"Oh, obviously they know that you *think* you know. But you are after all a poet, not a celestial navigator. I'll tell them that your data relates to a place which does not exist: that you believe the people to be snoozing on a planet at coordinates where there is no planet. Therefore, the Matrix must have misled you. However, I'll keep them occupied by saying that I've learnt enough from your mind – from, say, your memories of the night sky of this planet – to be able to locate it by comparative analysis with star charts of the various systems in and around the Twelve Circles." The Machine chuckled. "It could take weeks, and I'm quite likely to blow a fuse doing it."

"Can you ensure that no further harm comes to him?"

"I reckon."

"So be it."

You're not going? The voice of the Matrix, inhuman though it was, had penetrated the tempest of Dak's predicament like a beacon, something steady and enduring in an incredibly hostile place. He knew the impression of proximity was illusory, a mere electronic trick, but he had not expected the illusion to dissolve so quickly, or so coolly.

"Sorry – it's already gone." The Machine seemed considerably more sympathetic to his feelings than his old friend and tormentor, but it was the Matrix he wanted, as a child craves the moth-eaten plush of a familiar toy. "Never mind," said the Machine, reading his disappointment and taking no offence by it, "it won't be long now before you're home."

I don't know why we all refer to Earth as my home, thought Dak. I was born here, on Tok-ai-Do, I am a traitor to my own people.

"Some things are more important than patriotism."

Most things are more important than patriotism, Dak agreed glumly, but it's a lot easier being a member of a national club than a thinking individual. Life's tough on us citizens of the cosmos.

"You should try being a computer some time."

It's got to be better than this. When did anyone last feed you to a psychlops?

He felt again the impulse of sympathy; and suddenly and without any chain of logic knew that this was how the Machine destroyed its victims. By sympathy. By understanding them and humouring them and shouldering more and more of their burdens until nothing was left of the burden and nothing was left of them. The Machine absorbed them. Fear surged in him momentarily, then was itself absorbed. He heard the Machine say, "Do you understand what is meant by probability math?"

More or less.

"Simply, that although the alternatives at any junction are theoretically many and the combination thereof infinite, in practice the odds always tend to favour one option; so that a knowledgeable mathematician can, by calculating the likelihoods, predict future events with a degree of accuracy which must appear magical to the uninformed. Within the limits of the science, which of course excludes the effects of any unforeseeable factor, let me reassure you that the worst is over."

How about when you tell Honda I made a mistake?

"He won't hurt you. There would be no point, and he's not a cruel man. He's got nothing against you personally. He does what he considers an essential job with dedication and efficiency. He would consider vindictiveness unproductive, unethical and distasteful. Also, he likes you."

Dak felt a kind of hysteria bubbling through his brain. Then

Zen forbid I should ever get on the wrong side of him! There was a pause as he assimilated the conversation. You mean, you can predict the probable outcome of events which seem to me entirely unresolved?

"That's about it."

Then you know whether the Matrix will succeed. You know whether the sleepers will wake a free or subject people!

"I know the probabilities."

Which are?

"That the Matrix will succeed. That the people of Earth will be granted their freedom."

Although in the form in which he spoke with the Machine he had no body, only a mind, Dak was aware that he was trembling. It was one thing for a computer to know the future, quite another for a man. It was sacrilegious, too near an assumption of godhood. He felt it at once a miraculous bequest and an intolerable burden. When he found something to say it was, How sure are you?

The Machine laughed. "Men are the cleverest and most naive creatures in the known universe. Give them a horse and they check the teeth; give them gold and they bite it. Give them the future and they ask for a guarantee. I told you, it's a probability. It's more likely to happen that way than any of the other foreseeable ways. But it's still the future, and the future is by definition a state of flux. I can't promise you that no unsuspected factor won't intervene and send it off on a whole new probability train. I can't promise that no one will behave out of character at some fundamental juncture and make confetti of my calculations. All I can give you is a balance of odds. Probability."

Dak was obscurely glad. Obviously, he welcomed the news that the cause was not impossible, or already lost. But he didn't know if he could have coped with knowing the future as a certainty. It seemed to him it would take the point out of living. Without any resort to futurism he foresaw a situation in which, as the probability math developed, the only ones able to take advantage of its predictions would be computers, and since they never acted out of character the predictions would be self-fulfilling. There would be no future, only a temporal extension of the past.

"Don't be silly," the Machine said briskly. "Now, since we have to maintain a front if we're to convince anybody I've examined you, you'll have to stay a while longer. What do you want to do? Is there some memory you'd like to revisit? Some dream you'd like to act out? Perhaps you'd just like to sleep."

No, Dak thought quickly, next time I go to sleep I want it to be my idea.

"What, then? Your first sexual experience?"

No thanks, I don't feel up to farce.

"Can I ask you something?" The Machine had gone suddenly reticent.

Of course; though I wonder that you of all people need to ask permission.

"I'm not sectioning your brain for the answer to my inquisitiveness," responded the Machine indignantly. "All the same I would like to know and I think perhaps you can tell me."

I'll try.

"Well, as a computer I know all the biological angles to – um – sexual procreation and none of the emotional ones."

You want to know how it feels?

"Not exactly. It's just this. You both – um – disrobe; and – er – she lies down, and you lie down, kind of close; and you gaze into one another's eyes – um –"

Yes, Dak said, encouragingly.

"Well, what I want to know is – how do you stop yourselves from laughing?"

Peter Bassett, watching from the window, thought he saw some flicker of emotion cross Dak's passive white face. Afterwards he could not be sure, and anyway it was probably better not to wonder what was going on in his brain. Whatever it was would probably stop soon. For a man who had witnessed more dissolutions of personality than most, the doctor felt desperately sad at the loss of that free and gentle spirit whose existence he had only glimpsed after it was already too late. Honda had gone for a cup of tea, otherwise Bassett thought he might finally have blown his career and incurred serious physical injury by taking a swing at him.

Deep in the refuge of his mind no such dark thoughts troubled Dak. He was laughing, helplessly, drowning in a delicious sea of irresponsible mirth, while the Machine demanded plaintively, "You work with words – *why* can't you tell me what's so funny?"

Dak rose through the levels of consciousness like a languid fish, thoughts dipping and swooping like a seal making generally but unhurriedly for the surface. Savouring his encounter with the Machine, thinking about the Matrix and the task which lay ahead of it, relishing the last of that sensation of physical and emotional weightlessness which had come just in time to save his sanity, he accepted philosophically the gradual return of his body and with it the world.

"Time for you to go," the Machine had said, with apparent regret. "Take it slowly and quietly: the longer you sleep the better. Leave all the talking to me – you probably won't recall what's happened too clearly anyway. Tell them you remember nothing. They'll look after you. I'll keep them off your back, and the Matrix will be working to get you freed. Rest, trust and be patient."

Goodbye, said Dak.

"Goodbye . . ."

The twilight zone between sleeping and waking is an attractive one: like a virgin snowfield to a skier, like a blank page to a writer, it is the last lingering timelessness before the urge to create begins to make marks in the waiting white. It is a comfortable, uncluttered, uncomplicated country which one feels no great urgency to leave. But time has a way of catching up and at length, without having made any effort himself, Dak recognised that he was out of the twilight and into the day, and opened his eyes.

He was in a proper bed in a proper room, with no winking lights and no electric leads. Everything was white, but there were flowers on the locker. By the foot of the bed Dr Bassett was nodding in a chair, an open book unread in his lap.

"Are you waiting for me?" Dak was pleased to note that this slight breathiness of voice seemed the only hangover from his experience.

"Dak?" The doctor shot to his feet so fast that the book tumbled to the floor. He ignored it, stepping swiftly to the bedside, grabbing for his patient's pulse automatically, as a reflex action. "Are you all right?" He sounded incredulous.

Dak levered himself cautiously upright without provoking any adverse reaction. "I think so. When am I?"

"You've been unconscious for forty-eight hours. It's evening." Bassett was staring at him with an intensity which hardly constituted a bedside manner. "I don't understand. You look better now than when you went on that Machine."

"I've had two days' sleep."

"You've been comatose for two days. There IS a difference."

"It's all rest."

Bassett scowled. "Listen, Hamiko, Most people go on that Machine in reasonable shape and come off it in various forms of living death. Why should you do the opposite?"

"I followed your advice. I co-operated."

Bassett was squinting at him. "Really? It has to be the explanation. It's the only practical one. It's the only possible one. So, why don't I believe you?"

"Just a natural sceptic?"

"No." The doctor shook his head slowly. "My instincts are good. My morals are questionable, but my instincts are good." There was a light in his eye like a distant dawn breaking. "No, if I didn't know better I would conclude that that Machine chose to protect you. Chose. Of course, I know it's impossible. Computers, even very clever computers, have no discretion, and no pity. If I told my employers that I suspected their Machine of protecting you I would end up in this same hospital, in the next block along from this one, in a padded cell. So I am bound to accept your explanation. And I do. Just don't think I believe it."

"Everybody else does –?" It was half a statement, half a question.

"Yes." The stern lines of the doctor's face began to thaw. "Yes, they do. They take as gospel anything that tin god tells them. Well, if for once their god's taking them for a ride, I couldn't be more pleased."

Realising by now that as a liar he lacked talent, Dak dreaded a visit from Honda enquiring after his health and other things. But Honda didn't come. Instead he sent a present: Dak's guitar, from his quarters aboard *Leviathan*. The touch of his fingers on the strings awoke in Dak something that he thought had died. Life began to have a little charm again.

Though an improvement on his previous accommodation, it was a very strange hospital he was in: a kind of maximum security nursing-home for the violently insane. One man shrieked his insistence that he was God and had arrived on a tame comet; another that he was the abducted premier of a neighbouring planet.

"Not everybody here is mad," confided Peter Bassett. "For instance, you are not. Neither is the president of Xotl. But so long as most are, nobody believes the claims of the rest. Tell your nurse that you've been tortured by the authority of the government which also employs her. If she believed you she might be angry enough to do something about it. But she won't. She'll just smile and tuck you in and reach for another ampoule of paramorphine. In time you get conditioned: if you want to stay awake you don't mention what they consider your delusions. Consequently they think you're getting better. His Excellency the President hasn't learned that trick yet."

Among the actually mad were a number of inmates, men and women, whom Dak recognised as victims of the Machine. He did not know how he knew, for Bassett neither told him nor confirmed his suspicions, but he knew; as members of any exclusive club recognise one another instinctively. It was in their eyes – the desolation, the sense of having been robbed of something profoundly precious and not being able to remember what it was.

One such was Sayonara. Her name meant Goodbye, but it was not her name before she was raped by the Machine. She was small and frail, with long black hair framing a berry-brown face wide-eyed and vacant. "Like a shell-shocked pixie," said Dr Bassett. The only emotion she showed was fear, when someone approached her. She did not return to her quiet oblivion until they said "Goodbye" and went away. So she was called Sayonara.

"What did she do?" whispered Dak.

"To be given to the Machine?" Bassett looked at her, crouching empty-eyed in a corner of an empty room. "Rather more than you did, actually. There are people here we had no right to treat as we did, and others who only got what they deserved. If you can believe it, she's one of the latter. She's a terrorist. She plants bombs. She killed twenty-two people."

"You mean, she was a terrorist."

"Well, yes," admitted Bassett. "Since you put it that way. There isn't anything very terrible about her now, is there?"

"I find it all terrible," Dak said moodily. "What she's done, what you've done. This isn't my world – I don't know how I got into it. I don't know how long it will be before I start doing terrible things too." He looked at the floor, scuffing his toe disconsolately, then back at Bassett. "Who were the people she killed?"

"All sorts. Diners in a restaurant. Members of a theatre audience. Two were kids playing outside a shop: the plate-glass window scythed them down like a bloody harvest. One was an unborn baby, killed by shrapnel before it ever left the womb. Oddly enough, the mother survived – she really wasn't all that badly hurt."

"How did they find Sayonara?"

"She finally got one wrong and it went up while she was carrying it. Thing was, it was the last of a salvo of half a dozen, and nobody else knew where they were. She was in a coma: she couldn't have told us if she'd wanted to. We put her on the Machine while they were getting the theatre ready for surgery. We found the bombs, we repaired her body, but there was nothing we could do about her mind. All this happened five years ago. She's older than you, Dak, but to all intents and purposes she's a witless, frightened child of fourteen."

"Will she spend all her life here?"

"She couldn't live anywhere else."

"An ordinary hospital?"

"She's better off here. At least we understand how she got the way she is. If a method is ever found to reverse the effects of the

Machine, it'll be found here."

"Does she talk to nobody?"

"I don't think she can talk. She can't relate to people at all, can't bear anyone near her. She just wants to be alone; a cross between a hermit and a vegetable."

The fate of poor, stricken Sayonara, locked in her private void, visited only by the dread of other people, haunted Dak. Alone in his locked room through the long night his mind dwelt on her, and in the greater liberty of the day, supervised only by nurses and cruising medical bouncers on the look-out for hot-spots, he found himself drifting towards her lodgings in the women's ward.

Her room was much like his own, she had it to herself – only a few privileged or very sick inmates were not required to share – and she never left it. Although she had occupied it for five years there were no personal touches: no belongings on the locker, no posters on the wall, nothing but the glaring hospital-issue white. It was more like a monk's cell than either a hospital room or a prison.

She sat cross-legged in the corner, barefoot, hunched over, her eyes unfocused under the curtain of black hair. The door of her room stood ajar. An orderly opened it every morning and closed it again at night; except to facilitate the bringing and collecting of meal trays it might as well have been barred and shuttered, but the rules said daytime association between inmates should be encouraged so the door was dutifully opened each day before breakfast.

After watching for a long time from the corridor, Dak went into the room and quietly sat down cross-legged in the corner opposite the girl. Her eyes rolled wildly and she started to her feet like a startled animal; but Dak was very still, very unobtrusive, and after a while she settled back, ill at ease but without direction to her anxiety, as if aware that something was different but unable to isolate precisely what. As she scanned the room her blank gaze seemed to pass right through him.

He wanted to spend the night with her, observing and searching for a way into her locked-up mind, but the ward supervisor wouldn't hear of it and with the sound of their voices sending the girl into ape-like paroxysms of fear and anger he accepted a temporary defeat and returned to his own room, where they turned the key on him for the night. Despite its untimely termination he was not altogether displeased with his exploration. He had learned that Sayonara reacted much more violently to audible than to visual stimulae, and he had found she would tolerate his presence so long as he kept still and quiet. He went to sleep with half an idea as to the next step already forming in his head.

He was up and ready when the lights came on and his door was unlocked. Moving swiftly through the still quiet corridors he ambushed the breakfast trolley and hijacked trays for Sayonara and himself, balancing one on each hand like a trainee waiter.

The door was ajar. Inside the girl sat cross-legged in the corner, head down, her hair curtaining her face. Except that her shirt was now draped loosely around her thin body instead of tucked into her trousers, she might not have moved from the previous day. She responded to his appearance with a muted display of the same fear-aggression; muted, presumably, because it was morning, morning always brought breakfast and the person who brought breakfast always left promptly. Except today. Dak placed the girl's tray on the floor in front of her, with a solemn smile but no words, then retired to the far corner to eat his own meal, leaning the guitar up against the wall, where she could see it.

If in fact she could see, in the practical sense of the eyes telling the brain about the environment and the brain understanding. There was nothing wrong with Sayonara's eyes, but her apparent disinterest in the purely visual might have suggested some psychosomatic block between optic nerve and brain – hysterical blindness. Except that Dak was sure she was watching him. Covertly, without moving her eyes much less her head, and always from behind the dark Niagara of her hair; yet he felt intuitively that she was not only watching him but sizing him up, an encouraging thought because it presupposed some residue of intellect, some capacity for assessment, the ability to reach a decision. Of course, she would be aware of his presence by the sounds of him – his breathing, the rustle of his clothing, the absurd pantomime of trying to spread toast with a suicide-proof rubber knife – but it was significant that so far she had not reacted with violence. Hitherto all human noise had provoked such a reaction in her. Now it seemed that she had heard him near her, but because she recognised the quiet inoffensive presence of the previous day the reaction remained latent. He had no doubt that he could galvanise it by speaking, and he had no intention of making that mistake.

While he ate she made no move towards her own breakfast. When he finished and laid the tray quietly aside he felt her attention shift to the meal in front of her. She ate like an animal, in short, hurried snatches and without enjoyment, like an animal which knows it is vulnerable with its head down.

Dak reached for his guitar. At the first note the girl sat bolt upright, in neither fear nor anger for once but in surprise. In this place of strange sounds, all of them human, this was not recognisably a human sound. She stared at him – not with recognition, perhaps, but at least with interest. He had her attention without her paying for it in terror.

He was still excited when he talked to Peter Bassett ten hours later. "She listened to that guitar as if it were Orpheus's flute. Spellbound. She never moved for as long as I played, but after a while her eyes started to shine. She wouldn't let me stop: she began fretting every time I tried to take a breather. My arm's dropping off. She was communicating, Peter, or at least trying to, for the first time in – what, five years? I'm going to see her again tomorrow, see if she'll let me sing to her. Peter, suppose I can get her to sing back –?"

Dak, looking up with something like wine flashing in his eyes, realised his enthusiasm was not being returned in kind. Dr Bassett was regarding him from under low brows. "Dak, I don't want you messing around with this girl."

"Messing around?" Dak was stung. "Well, call it what you like, I seem to have achieved more with Sayonara in forty-eight hours than your medical scientists have in five years. I'm not hoping to take advantage of her, if that's what you think."

"It's not, and you know it. I know you mean well, Dak. I agree you seem to have found some kind of key to her isolation. But you don't know enough about the forces and factors involved. I can't let you continue."

"Why not?" demanded Dak.

"Because for one thing the trustees of this hospital have their doubts about one loonie treating another," snapped Bassett. He drew a deep breath. "And then – think what it is you're doing. If you succeed, you'll make her completely dependent on you. Yes, you'll give her a window on the world: you'll *be* her window. What happens when you leave? You're not going to be here for the next ten years, the next twenty years, the way she is. When you go you'll slam the window shut on her again, and this time she'll know all about it. Now she's in limbo. There's nothing good about that, but at least she's past despair. Don't give her hope and then wrench it away again. Don't teach her to feel only to appreciate the desolation you'll return her to. You think music will help her? All right, I'll try it. *I* will; because if it comes to anything I can give her time and stability, and you never can."

Dak was flattened and a little hurt by the doctor's attitude but not blind to his argument. Conceding with a faintly bad grace he said, "Suppose she won't respond to you – or anyone she associates with this mausoleum and what's been done to her here? Surely any progress is better than none?"

"For whom? For medical science, for my reputation, for your self-esteem, possibly. But not for Sayonara. For her ignorance isn't bliss but it is a dire necessity. If she can't be something like human, and the Machine may have deprived her of that potential irrevocably, she needs to be oblivious. You might as well say I should stop anaesthetising patients because they've a right to their pain. If Sayonara wasn't in a mental stupor as a result of her condition I should probably have to drug her. You don't know what's going on in her mind; yet, full of reforming zeal and righteous indignation, you're prepared to make her face it alone. Stop tampering, Dak. Write her a poem, you're qualified for that, but stop playing around with her mind."

"All right, all right," growled Dak, "you've made your point. But, Peter, see her. See if you can't do something for her."

"Tomorrow. I'll go make music for her tomorrow. But it'll have to be the clarinet – I don't play guitar."

"Shall I come with you?"

"No."

Remaining conscientiously in his room, Dak didn't hear the clarinet or anything else, but he became aware of a tension in the air which, possibly because of his own preoccupation, he associated with the women's wing. The staff wouldn't speak to him, hurrying by on mysterious missions, and none of the inmates he spoke to understood what he was talking about.

When Peter Bassett finally came to his room after midday there was blood on his shirt and a dressing at his throat. "You and your bright ideas!" He flopped into the chair, exhausted and depressed.

"Whatever happened?"

"I guess she must prefer folk to classical. She tried to kill me. She stabbed me with a plastic fork." Dak was staring with undisguised horror, but Bassett saw a certain humour in the situation. "It would take a loonie to try and commit murder with disposable cutlery. Oh, cheer up, Dak, it could have been worse – she might have got her hands on a rubber axe –"

"Are you all right?"

"Yeah. Just four little holes in the middle of a bruise."

"What about her?"

"She's under sedation. She was practically foaming at the mouth for a while there. Poor cow."

"What went wrong, Peter?"

"Nothing went wrong. It happened just as you said it would. Music unlocked the door on a bit of her personality and she started to communicate. Unfortunately, we both forgot why she was here in the first place – that her personality is anarchical and her chosen method of communication was violence. She reverted to type, with the added complication that she is now brain-damaged so she cannot exercise even basic discrimination in her use of violence. She is profoundly psychopathic."

Dak shook his head, moved and miserable. "What happens now?"

Bassett shrugged. "A lot depends on how she is when the sedative wears off. If she's safely back in her shell, we're back where we started – which may not be good, but it could sure as hell be a lot worse. But if she comes out fighting we're in trouble. If we can't control it any other way, we'll have to consider surgery."

"Surgery?"

"Amigdolotomy. The amigdola is, or more accurately appears to be, the seat of aggression in the brain. Amigdolotomy is a form of psychosurgery in which the amigdola is destroyed. The patient wakes up without anger; virtually without emotion. It's an effective last resort in cases of uncontrollable psychotic aggression, but I wouldn't use it to prevent – for instance – the occasional black eye. It's too much like turning people into androids."

Dak was still staring at him, his eyes enormous. His voice threatened to break. "Peter, I'm *sorry*. I don't know how – You warned me. You told me not to tamper with something I didn't understand. I thought I knew better. I thought, a poet understands people better than a doctor. And now in my ignorance and my arrogance I've hurt you and destroyed her. Zen knows the Machine didn't leave her much, but I've left her with less. If there's anything I can do –" He could not continue.

Bassett's tone was gentler. "Come on, Dak, it's unfortunate but it's not the end of the world. She was no treasure to begin with: who knows, when this is all over she may be better off than before."

"Forgive me," whispered Dak Hamiko, but Dr Bassett could not have said to whom the plea was addressed.

An hour later he marched back into the doctor's office, came to attention on the carpet and said, "I want half an hour with the Machine."

Bassett stared at him. "You want what?"

"I want to talk to the Machine. It got her that way, maybe it knows how to put her right only no one's cared enough to ask."

"It's not the Oracle, Dak, it's an instrument of cerebral dissemination. It doesn't heal people, it pulls them apart."

"I know that. And you know that the Machine and I have an

understanding. Perhaps it can't help, but the only way I can find out is by asking. You can arrange it."

"I can't!"

"Of course you can. This hospital is under your authority."

"The Machine isn't. It belongs to the security services. You want to ask Honda?"

"It isn't in use all the time?"

"No," the doctor agreed doubtfully.

"Then you can sneak me in there while there's nobody about."

"It takes a highly trained team to use that thing."

"You can manage."

"Dak, you're asking me to perform an operation single-handed!"

"It's been done before."

"Not this one, it hasn't. You'd need prepping, the electrodes have to be implanted, there are monitors to watch –"

"Does any of it have to be done simultaneously?"

"Yes. No. I don't know. It's out of the question."

"Hello again," said the Machine brightly. "Are you in more trouble?"

No, said Dak, but I've got someone else in plenty.

"Thank God that's over," Bassett said fervently when Dak opened his eyes. "I've been sitting here in a cold sweat waiting for you to wake up. You're all right, are you? Every time I heard steps in the corridor I thought Honda was on my tail. You'll be the death of me if I can't get rid of you soon. Breathe deeply – that's right. I don't know why I let you get me into these things. I was perfectly happy with my career until you came along: now you've got me conspiring to pervert the course of justice, poaching their Machine, aiding and abetting an enemy of the State – I'm sure you are an enemy of the State, aren't you?"

"Peter."

"What?"

"It isn't over yet. You're going to have to aid and abet me again."

"Oh, God," moaned Bassett. "I can't take much more of this. It's wreaking havoc with my digestion, and look at these hands – they haven't shaken like this since I first went solo."

"And this time it could be difficult –"

"This time!"

"– because you'll have both me and Sayonara to plug in and watch simmering. Can you arrange it?"

"I'm not hearing this," decided the doctor. "I'm not hearing any of this. I'm going home. I suggest you do the same, in so far as the rooms here can be so described, and if anyone sees you on the way, stick out your arms and pretend you're sleep-walking." He made for the door with every appearance of determination.

Dak said mildly, "I don't think I can walk yet."

Bassett stopped, looking down at him for some moments before answering. "No, I suppose not. You'd better come to my office, it's nearer. Give me your arm. While you're getting your breath back you can tell me exactly what the Machine said."

Dak didn't – not exactly. He told the doctor that a three-way communication between the girl, the Machine and himself as intermediary was Sayonara's only chance of a normal life, and Bassett – having twice seen Dak emerge unscathed from his encounters with the Machine – didn't think to ask if it was dangerous. Dak said the Machine's terrible skill would enable his mind to gently untangle the twisted skeins of the girl's; the Machine's warning that he might become enmeshed in them and drown in her madness he kept to himself. For he did not wish to be debarred from his expiation of guilt, and he needed Peter Bassett's help, yet he viewed the endeavour with deep trepidation.

"You came, then?" said the Machine when he emerged from the brief bedlam dark of transition. "I wasn't sure you would."

I wasn't sure that I would; only that I should.

"Not that it isn't nice to see you again. It is. In my line of work you don't often meet people twice. Only the Matrix'll fry me if it ever finds out what we're doing."

There's nothing more I can do for the Matrix or the people. Perhaps I can do something for this girl.

"Okay, it's your brain. Now, you know what you're looking for?"

Not really. You said I'd know when I found it. I didn't find that particularly helpful.

"Sorry, kid, best I can do. You see, there are no absolutes. What you find in there depends on you and her. Subjectively, you're embarking on a journey: it may be through a maze, or a tunnel, or along trails in a wilderness – I don't know, it's in the hands of your imagination. Objectively you're going nowhere – just lying comatose on that table. But while your mind is exploring hers it'll supply some rational scenario. What you have to find depends on what form that rationalisation takes – but you'll know, once you're in there. If you stay in the mainstream of her subconscious and don't allow yourself to be distracted, sooner or later you'll come on the nucleus of her disturbance – whatever it was that so damaged her psyche that she could never afterwards escape its consequences. If you can break through that scar tissue she may be able to rebuild herself, be complete."

I understand.

"I doubt it, but then it's not necessary that you should. The most important thing for you to remember is not to get lost. If you stray off into her crazy emotions you'll never get back. If your imagination presents you with a path, follow it, slavishly; if a ladder, climb it. Ignore everything else. When it brings you to a climax, tackle it: open the box, bulldoze through the brick wall, defeat the dragon, whatever. If you're successful you'll have no trouble getting back. If not, I honestly don't know. Now, are you ready?"

Thank you for your help.

"Thank me when you get back. Good luck."

Childe Roland to the dark tower came, Dak thought, perhaps unwisely, and his world turned over.

Chapter Six

There was no hoary cripple to point a way, but the plain which stretched before him was as grim as Browning's; sparsely carpeted with the limp yellow grass which grows under abandoned lawnmowers, featureless into the far distance and sodden underfoot – not like the grateful recipient of rain, more like an imperfectly drained bog. A lowering grey sky shot with purple bathed the whole in a leprous light.

Remembering the Machine's injunction Dak looked around for a path. There was none, neither path nor track, and the only signs of passage on the adjacent ground were his own pooling footprints. Looking at them, the corner of his eye seemed to register some movement far off across the plain. He snapped his gaze sharply in that direction but failed to discern either movement or feature. Still, he had nothing else do. When he was sure no path offered itself he turned his face to the perhaps imagined movement on the horizon and began to walk. The wet ground sucked at his feet and made dismal slurping sounds as he tracked over it, and he cursed himself for not thinking of primrose paths and leafy glades in those last vital moments before the Machine switched him through.

He had no concept of time, except that the more of it that passed the wearier he became, but at length the joyless introspection into which he had by degrees retired as a refuge from his dreary trek was interrupted by two realisations: that the plain was a plain no longer, its limits having closed in in the form of converging escarpments channelling the flatland ever narrower between them; and that it was growing darker. He stopped, for the first time, to take stock of the situation. He had not seen a sun at all, could not judge its position, but the light was fading perceptibly. It might see him another mile or two but after that he would be in the dark, and he had no idea how long such a night might last.

On the other hand, the appearance of the rocky crests marching on either side of him like petrified armies gave him hope. The plain was not, then, eternal – a kind of water-logged limbo. It had shape, and therefore probably also purpose. It occurred to him that the funnelling effect of the scarps turned the plain itself into a kind of path, which would become more defined the farther he followed it. But path or no, he dared not continue beyond nightfall.

This time he was looking right at it when the movement was repeated. It was directly ahead, on the very edge of his diminishing vision, yet not so far that he could form no opinion as to what caused it. It seemed to him like a flutter of clothing, the flourish of a cloak or the flounce of a girl's dress in the wind. Without pausing to think he picked up his weary heels and gave chase.

The girl fled; the light fled; Dak ran until the blood roared in his ears, until his heart threatened to beat its way out of his confining breast, until his muscles cracked and screamed; until his feet disappeared from under him. In the all-but-darkness he did not see the terrain's sudden plummet but some faint residual instinct shrieked a warning, too late; in the instant of braking, his feet hit scree, the scree moved under him and, a stony whirlwind of shale and flailing limbs, he shot into space.

"None of this is real," he told himself firmly, clawing his way back from oblivion. "Her psyche may hurt me but it can't injure me: my body is safely back in Peter Bassett's clinic." With a conscious effort of belief he uncurled himself from the foetal ball, cautiously stretching limbs he found stiff but intact, and amid a clatter of falling stones rose slowly to his feet.

Before him was a building: a tower, narrow, tall and dark. The girl was watching him from the doorway, illuminated by the last of the sun's rays striking into the hollow. As he saw her she moved through the portal and shut the door, and the sun went out.

Roland blew a horn, and what happened after that is not recorded. Dak groped his way to the great wooden door and, seeing no reason to depart from civilised behaviour, tapped upon it with his knuckles. The door swung inward on silent hinges. Dak followed the girl's mind into its stonghold.

Outside the tower was high and narrow and dark. Inside it was vast, brilliant. He entered a mirror-maze of jewel-faceted splendour, lights and colours and reflections chasing across the hard brightness of a myriad screens, confusing, entrancing, alarming.

The movement of his body between the crystal walls sent battalions of images, dissected, discrete, flickering down the avenues in unexpected patterns, for what he thought were mirrors were passages and where he thought there was space he met glass. As his hands groped for something stable, a continuity, blind by virtue of not too few but too many stimulae crowding his eyes, the mirrors sang, as if they were not fixed but free to brush together like wind-chimes, producing vibrant, alien notes of triumph and mayhem: an insane gloriana. The music was like the colours that flashed with such excessive brilliance in the crystal facets: exquisite to the point of pain, maddening, and unutterably sinister.

A flat whine like a mosquito impinged on his awed awareness and half a step behind him one of the plates shattered into a jewelled fountain of fragments – sequins which showered his clothes and stung his skin like windblown sand. A second mosquito plucked urgently at his sleeve, but he was diving for the illusory safety of a sparkling corner when the third bored a needle-fine hole through the mirror which had held his image the moment before, turning it into a crazy-paving of distorted memories. As he fled, chased on every side by dancing mimicries, he had no clear idea what was happening except that the girl's insanity was fighting back.

Common sense catching up with his flying form, he realised he was being panicked into a showdown in somebody else's backyard, on terms that were anything but equable. The maze might funnel him towards some dead-end killing ground and he would have no way of knowing until he was trapped. Reason dictated that inside her own head the girl could not but win any direct confrontation. Panting, not only with exertion, Dak ground to a halt and faced back the way he had come.

There was nothing to see, only the shimmering crystal with its mocking panoply: infinite platoons of diminishing yellow men in black clothes, perfectly drilled, moving in daunting unison. The nearer of them had hollow, cadaverous faces and suspicious animal eyes, and they bent slightly over heaving breasts, as if ready to take flight again at an instant's notice. Displeased with this crude, unyielding portrait of himself, Dak forced his body to straighten up and his head to lift, though all his instincts chid him for increasing the target he presented. He said, "I want to help you."

The response was immediate: the whine, a spark, and a sensation as of a white-hot skewer thrust into his thigh. He gasped, as much with shock as with pain, and clutched at the wound with spastic fingers that found no blood, only a small charred hole in his trouser-leg and a fiery spot he couldn't bear to touch.

"I don't need help." The voice was not recognisably a girl's. Primordial, savage, atavistic, it held the ring of much more than one lifetime's murder. Pain beating in his blood, Dak finally recognised his enemy: the unborn, undying Lucifer of the human spirit who finds little expression in a normal soul but who had made of the girl Sayonara a playground. "I don't need you. It was unwise of you to come."

A second spark blazed beside the first, so close that the charred circles in the black acetate fused together. Dak fell heavily to his knee as the injured leg gave under him, his shoulder crashed against the mirror and he held himself there by the palms of his hands flat against the glass, which was not cold but subtly, indecently warm. He tasted salt and realised he had bitten through his lip to keep from crying out. He wiped the blood from his mouth with the back of a hand. An unholy chuckle reverberated along the crystal corridors.

He reacted with inexplicable, marvellous anger, a vibrant surge of fury against the unseen daemon threatening him. Even a worm will turn, but man is often at his brilliant best *in extremis*. Faced with the apparent certainty of death, his soul or his temper may be stirred by something quite trivial and irrelevant, and in this irrational whirlwind of passion the most unlikely men become heroes. Dak had no thought of heroism, and in his own mind he was already lost, but his manhood rebelled against a crouching animal's death at the whim of a tormentor who laughed as she killed. Without wondering whether his leg would support him he flung himself to his feet, cast around wildly for the object of his anger and finding no one, turned on the glittering mirror and put his fist clean through it.

For an instant it hung, shivering, around his wrist like a great bracelet; then the shimmering shards fell and flew apart, momentarily filling the air, and a black hole appeared where the mirror had flashed. He dived through it, into oblivion.

After the brilliant glare of the mirrors the darkness seemed impenetrable. But blindness in an unknown element was preferable to a death he could see coming, spark by spark, in a battalion of mocking crystals; beating the empty air he plunged on, dragging his stiffening leg behind him. That he heard no sound of pursuit did not entirely reassure him that there was none.

A line appeared in the blackness, a dull grey oblique stretching up through the otherwise featureless dark. He made for it. If nothing else it held the prospect of some relief for his starved eyes.

The grey line was a rail, a stair-rail trailing aloft, he couldn't see where; but there was light, a long way up, a yellow kerb such as might appear under a door. Holding the dull metal rail in one hand and steadying his trembling thigh with the other he looked up and tried to gain some impression of distance. He could not, but the height of the yellow strip above his head and the soft imprecision of its light said it was a long way for a man with two holes in his leg. "It would have to be stairs," he observed wearily to himself as he began to climb.

He almost didn't make it. It was a very close-run thing, and entropy almost won. His injured leg gave out before he was halfway. He continued for some time, dragging himself up by the rail; later again he climbed like an animal, on hands and knee, like a lame dog. Half a dozen times, with his shoulders cracking, his ribs heaving over the tumult of his lungs, with the sweat pouring into his eyes and down his flanks and chilling him as it flowed, he fell upon his face on the hard stair in the conviction that he would never move again. The last time he collapsed scant paces from the door: he could see it quite plainly if he wiped the sweat from his eyes and forced them to stay open, and ignored the shooting red lights like rockets at a carnival. And he propped his chin on his wrist, too exhausted to hold up his head, and looked at the iron-banded wood above the yellow threshold, and was quite sure he would die before he could reach it.

He could never afterwards remember how he made that final assault: as a man, as an animal, or crawling on his belly like a snake. His next conscious recollection was of lying curled on his side before the door, his left eye pressed against the yellow crack and watering from the draught. When it occurred to him that someone might open the door and find him there, like something dragged up by an incredibly determined cat, he felt around for his legs, somehow got them under him, and rose unsteadily to his feet. He cast a last look down the infinite stairs, disappearing into the darkness below, then turned back to the door.

Dak, although an oriental, was a gentleman at least. He knocked before entering.

The room was like a tower-room in a mediaeval masque, with lancet windows glazed with horn, rich hangings around the circular wall, skins on the floor. The girl said, "Come in. I've been expecting you."

The voice was calm, clear, articulate, the self-possessed voice of a girl come to womanhood, but it issued from the figure of a child: a child of twelve or fourteen years flame-clad in opulent silks and mounted on a throne.

Dak mumbled, "I don't understand –" then swayed so violently that the child sprang from her dais to his side, taking his arm and guiding him to the couch which was the only other furniture in the room. No loom? he wondered vaguely; no web, no mirror?

"I think you had better sit down," said the child. "Where are you hurt?"

"My leg," he said. "Who –?"

"Yes, I see," she interrupted. "She's depressingly accurate with that weapon, you know. You're lucky you escaped when you did. It's toxic, it works on the nerves: her next hit would have had you climbing the walls, the one after that would have killed you."

"I don't see how I can be killed by a weapon which is a figment of your imagination," Dak said, a shade sullenly.

"Oh – oh, I see, we have a thinker here. Well, tell me, philosopher, didn't it hurt when her ray pierced your flesh?"

"It did, of course," he agreed reluctantly.

"And now you feel exhausted and rather sick?"

"The stairs –"

"She shot you, it hurt, you began to feel weak and quickly lost the use of your leg; now your muscles aren't responding as they should and your sense of balance is affected. An illusion? In here, philosopher, you, too, are a figment of my imagination, as subject to the laws which govern this place as anything you see. Do you know of the faith-healer from Deal?"

He stared groggily. "Where's Deal?"

She ignored him. "He remarked, 'Although pain isn't real, if I sit on a pin and it punctures my skin I dislike what I fancy I feel.' Let's have no more nonsense about your invulnerability – I doubt if you believe it any more than I do. If you really imagine you got here unscathed, I'll fetch you a mirror."

"I don't care," Dak mumbled, leaning his head against the back of the couch and letting his eyes close, "if I never see another mirror as long as I live."

He must have slept for a time. Perhaps it was the effects of the imagined toxin. He found himself on his back with one of the skin rugs across him which for a moment he thought was the living beast. He started up, and the child said from her throne, "You're safe here. She cannot come. If she could, I would not exist."

"Can you explain?" He pushed the rug off him and found a gaudy banner of silk around his thigh where she must have bound it while he slept. He grinned, and she smiled in reply.

"She is my future, as I am her past. Lacking a common present we can never meet. We diverged at puberty, when her brute passions became too powerful for my intellect to control. As one we were an unstable equation, so we became two. I continued to develop only mentally, she only physically. She is the one you knew before. Incidentally, I enjoyed your music."

He shook his head, bewildered. "How – why – did she overpower you? Was there some cause – some single reason?"

"A catalyst? None that I recall; no trauma. I think she – my primitive half – just happened to be stronger than I. When I could fight her no more I withdrew here, leaving her the field. I'm sorry she wrought so much havoc before she could be stopped. You shouldn't have come here, you know. She isn't worth trying to save."

"Perhaps not. I don't know. But what about you?"

The child laughed, almost gaily. "Me? I can't leave. I opted out, I can't get back now I've lost control of this continuum too. No, I'll have to take what she brings on us."

"Look," Dak said honestly. "I don't know if I can get either of us away safely, but I have to try and get back and I'd like you to come with me. I have a friend – who enabled me to come here in the first place – who may be able to help you. Minds are his business, I know he'll do what he can. He – it's a machine I'm talking about, the Machine."

"I know," said the child softly.

"It's a gamble, I know, I can't promise we'll succeed or even survive, but at least it's a chance of freedom, and you haven't much of a future here, have you?"

The eyes of Oshi Wan Sei, which is who she was before she became Sayonara, were large and deep and full of a yearning sorrow. "Dak Hamiko," she said quietly, "you have been alone, but not quite alone, not for ten years. Do you think this room could be anything but a velvet cage from which any escape, even into death itself, would be a blessed journeying?"

"You'll come with me?"

"If I can, for as far as I can."

There could be no escape for Oshi Wan Sei through the marquisite maze of her *alter ego*, so Dak looked for another way out. He opened one of the horn windows. Below was impenetrable night.

"What's below?"

"I've never looked."

His eyebrows climbed. "Never?"

"This is my prison – my world. Until you came there was no outside."

"Well, there's one now. I can hear waves."

They tore all the hangings, all the brilliant silks into strips of which they wove a rope. Dak tested it for strength and, fingers crossed, judged it fit. He lowered then recovered it but the end was not wet. He weighted the end and tried again, with the same result.

"There's a lot of line here, but not enough to reach the water," he said, summing up their situation. "I don't know how far it falls short. Perhaps only a handspan, in which case we're home and dry – well, not that exactly, of course, but you know what I mean. Alternatively, this tower may be built on the edge of a cliff dropping sheer Phaeton knows how far to the sea. If the sea comes deep to the foot of the drop we could take a fall, perhaps even a long fall. But if there are rocks, or we hit the beach, even a short fall could be too far. Also, there may be a savage tide, or sharks, or for some reason I haven't thought of we may be unable to swim in a figment of your imagination." They both smiled. "Once we're on that rope we're committed – even if it doesn't break. If we get to the bottom and it's no good, we shan't be able to climb up again. We have to decide this side of the window-sill. What shall we do?"

Oshi Wan Sei threw the particoloured flag from the lancet a third time. "Start climbing," she said matter-of-factly, "and praying to the spirits of our ancestors."

Her courage was the courage of a woman, but her body was that of a child, with a child's frailty: Dak doubted her ability to cling to the silken web if the wind should snatch them, so with fragments of remaining silks he made a harness and set her on his back. "Hold tight, and don't be afraid if we start to spin. At the bottom of the rope we'll let go together, but push yourself away from me – there's no point in us breaking each other's limbs. And if you make it and I don't – good luck."

"And if you make it and I don't – thank you," she said.

With the child on his shoulders, the silk cutting into his hands and the wind threatening to tear them from the face of the tower, Dak crabbed his way slowly down the dark stone, grateful for its roughness. He had wondered how his injured leg would serve, but if anything its stiffness was an advantage – it was the only part of him that didn't go wobbly at the thought of what waited below.

The farther down the flogging silk, the greater the effect of the wind. He lost his footholds for seconds at a time, spinning helplessly in the raging ether, unable to do more than cling desperately to the flailing line and hope his feet would find the stone before his head or the child's did. After they were launched on the perilous descent he never wondered if the silk would hold: that was a matter entirely beyond his knowledge and influence. But while it held, every minute brought them closer to safety; or, rather, to safety or oblivion.

The climb took an increasing toll of his dwindling strength, and the end of the line came just in time as his hands, the clenching muscles in the forearms exhausted, began to lose their grip. Still it came as a shock when the end of the pennant whipped up in his face. He tightened his grasp in momentary panic, then bent the fall around his hands for a last respite.

"This is it," he shouted into the wind. "Are you ready?"

For answer he felt the frail arms hug his neck, and a cold face buried itself against his skin. "Thank you for my freedom," Oshi Wan Sei said in his ear.

He took a deep breath, kicked away from the tower and let go the line.

One thing about this job, he thought irreverently, taking in his surroundings in the first languid appraisal of returning consciousness, you never get waking in the same bed two mornings running. He tried to remember where he was and failed, so he tried to remember how he came here and that was a blank too. It wasn't the Machine room or his own room, or the interrogation room, or – No, it wouldn't be the girl's throne-room. The tower didn't exist any more.

Wherever it was, things had taken a turn for the better while he was away. There were curtains at the window, carpet on the floor, a video/MC in the corner, and the door had a lock on the inside, which suggested it hadn't one on the outside. His bag and his guitar were stacked beside the dresser. Attached to the guitar was a bright pseudosilk strap, a gaudy banner. It had always been there, but for some reason it meant something extra now. Memory began to stir, but before it could crystallise, sleep caught up with him, laid hold on and pervaded him, and left him with only a tiny crease between the narrow brows above his shut eyes.

He next roused to the sound of his name and the figure of Peter Bassett standing over him. The doctor had shed his white coat and his mobile face was set in grave lines. "Dak," he said again, "it's time to wake up."

"Coming," yawned Dak, sitting up and forcing his eyes into focus. "Hello. What's the panic, I was only sleeping it off?"

"While you've been sleeping it off, things have been happening round here, rather fast." He paused, chewing his lip. "First, do you know that the girl died?"

"Ah," Dak murmured, and said nothing more for a minute. "No, I didn't know, but perhaps I should have. She said goodbye to me. I think possibly she knew she couldn't get away. She was glad to die. Her body was a prison to her, her condition a torment. She thanked me for her freedom."

Bassett sat down heavily on the end of the bed. "Next you'll tell me we did her a favour."

"Yes," Dak said seriously. "Yes, I think we did. Granted that she was what she was, and the Machine had already had a go at her, I think she's better off now than she was a week ago. I think she'll think so."

Bassett shook his head, almost angrily. "In your own way you're as ruthless as Honda is."

"Am I? Perhaps I am. I'm sorry she's dead, but I cannot regret that she's no longer living the life she was when I first saw her. She had long exhausted all the pleasure she was going to get out of this existence. I don't know what follows death, but if it's oblivion then she's found peace and if it's anything more then she has to be happier now than she was."

When the doctor spoke again it was at a tangent. "Was it bad – inside?"

"For me, you mean? Yes, it was. I can't say why, exactly. It was very strange. I was often frightened, sometimes hurt, but the worst thing was the exhaustion. All the time I seemed to be pushing against invisible forces, wanting to stop and knowing that if I did I'd never get back. Like a bad dream at the moment you realise it's not a dream and you're not going to wake up."

Finally Bassett smiled, the friendship Dak valued making its come-back in his eyes. "Welcome back."

"Back where?"

Bassett looked round the room. "That's right, you don't know. That's the other part of the news. This is the closest approximation this hospital can offer to VIP accommodation. You've been elevated from the status of inmate to that of guest. A directive from the Secretariat of the Alliance. God knows how they came to know about you but they do; also the sleepers. As soon as you can travel you're to address the Senate on Pax Mundi."

Chapter Seven

The Senate offered him an Embassy caravel, and the Planetary State of Tok-ai-Do proffered a battle-cruiser. Unless someone else had claimed it, he said, he already had a ship. He did not know what his destination would be on leaving Pax Mundi but he preferred self-sufficiency to being a passenger aboard a borrowed craft. Tok-ai-Do agreed to release *Leviathan* to him on condition – it wasn't put quite like that – that she carry a Navy crew. Dak acccpted readily enough, confident that if necessary he could ditch them on Pax Mundi under the protection of the Senate.

Peter Bassett came also. Dak asked him to and Bassett accepted, both knowing and neither saying that it would be unsafe for him to remain after the eyes of the Senate shifted away. Beautiful, civilised, peaceful Tok-ai-Do had become a snake-pit under the surface. Perhaps it had always been and Dak, comfortable and safe within the system, had not suspected.

Dak wanted to contact the Matrix but he didn't know how to do it safely so he waited for the Matrix to contact him. Once his plans were settled he moved his belongings back into Sharm's cabin and began sleeping there.

The call came, like God's to Samuel, in the middle of the night; and, like Samuel, he did not immediately recognise it for what it was. Roused from sleep by the muffled sound of a voice his first thought was of intruders, his second – more rational – that some piece of equipment had been left on by the engineers who had spent the day assessing the ship's space-fitness, and his third that he should go and see what is was. He found a watch-light on the flight-deck, the communications system plainly active although the switches were off, and no sign of anyone but himself on board. He moved cautiously across the deck on silent, naked feet.

Then a strident metallic voice laced with complaint announced caustically, "Dak Hamiko, if you do not respond to this communication very soon I shall have The Machine instruct the Chief of Security to instruct the Officer of the Watch to instruct one of his patrols to come round there and knock you up."

Dak rushed to the console and snatched up the microphone as a man might reach for his best friend's hand. "If you're so incomparably clever," he said by way of greeting, "how come you don't know it's the middle of the night?"

"You would prefer to talk in the day, when you are surrounded by State spies and lackeys?"

"How did you know I was sleeping here?"

"I am –"

"– The Matrix," they finished in unison. Dak grinned. "I know it's only vibrating tinfoil, but it's good to hear your voice."

"Are you all right now?"

"Fine. Quite fine. The Machine took the pressure off, and the directive from Pax Mundi made them release me. But what in Zen," he demanded worriedly, "does the Senate want to see me for? What can I tell them that you can't?"

"Nothing," the Matrix agreed baldly. "Not as much, in fact. But for some reason best known to themselves they do not care to hear submissions from other than carbon-based organisms. I approached them as you suggested with a digest of what was about to happen to the people. They – the Secretariat – said the people would have to speak for themselves, they could not accept evidence from a watch-dog computer. I said the people could not speak for themselves because they were asleep. I said that the fact that they were asleep was fundamental to the entire issue. I said that if the people were awake and thus able to speak for themselves there would be no need for them to do so, and not only would they not need a watch-dog computer, they would not need help from the Alliance either."

Dak half heard the acrimonious exchange. "What did they say

to that?"

The Matrix sounded affronted. "That machines could not act as counsel. That our logic gave us an unfair disadvantage over human advocates and shifted the balance of justice from the humane to the legalistic. They meant that we would do the Senate out of a job, since prosecuting and defending computers inevitably reaching the same conclusion would obviate the need for a jury. Do you not find," it added irascibly, "that humans can be terribly arrogant?"

"You mean, in view of the fact that we are less perfect than yourself?"

"Quite." Then it said again, but more softly, more knowingly, "Quite. Dak Hamiko, I have missed you."

They talked at length. Dak was anxious lest the signal be intercepted and traced, not to him but to the Matrix, but it dismissed the possibility scathingly. "Do you suppose I need the assistance of the General Telephone Company to speak to you? There are no more than four computers in the Alliance capable of tracing this frequency, the only one in the Sixth Circle is the Machine, and we both know whose side the Machine is on."

"Do you know about Probability Math?" asked Dak.

"Of course. Probability – Ah," it said then, understanding. "The Machine has computed probability regarding the people."

"Well, regarding your success."

The great remote computer seemed to sniff. "Probability Math has a number of prophets, among which we may number the Machine, and an approximately equal quota of sceptics, including myself. It is an attractive theory, but while its predictions can be upended by every chance variable it is hardly due the status of a science. The plain fact is that, given that an event is possible, there are two alternatives regarding it. It either will happen or it will not, and there is little point designating one of them a probability when, from the moment the choice is made, it is neither science nor theory but history."

"The Machine thinks you'll win."

"I intend to win; but I prefer to stake my faith in your ability to move the Senate than in a jumble of figures thrown up by the

Machine's cosmic dice. Go back to sleep now. I want you in good order when you put my case before the Alliance."

"We don't leave for two days," protested Dak.

"You need to be fit by then. How did you hurt your leg?"

Dak started and looked down at it guiltily, stuck out in front of him because it was still too stiff to bend easily. "How do you know about my leg?"

"The Machine. The garrulous instrument made such a point of saying how trivial an injury it was that I suspected it of trying to cover something up. What have you been doing?"

"It's nothing. A little stiffness, that's all. I got it – er – sleep-walking." He rubbed the slowly fading numbness where the imaginary weapon had stung his astral flesh and remembered the chill which had smote him with the realisation, coming fast on his return to consciousness, that his real body had been no safer under Peter Bassett's gaze than the phantom form which clothed his exploring mind.

"I think you had better return here as quickly as you can," said the Matrix. "You are obviously not safe out in the universe alone."

"You can say that again," Dak agreed fervently, but the Matrix didn't. The Matrix was gone.

While there was work to be done, preparations to make, Dak was fully occupied and had no time to think about the confrontation ahead. But when the preparations were complete and no longer filled his waking hours, the enormity of the task wished on him by the Matrix bore in upon him, striking him rigid with shock and foreboding. By their joint attitudes the Matrix and the Senate had put on his shoulders the future of a world and all its inhabitants. It had lain there before, of course, but then the issues had been clear-cut. If he had betrayed the people under Honda's quiet torture he would have broken his promise to the Matrix. His position then was invidious but simple: he knew where he stood. Now, though his object remained the same, much more was demanded of him than mere endurance. He would have to pit his wits and whatever oratorial skill he possessed against the cleverness and incisive scrutiny of the Alliance's statesmen, also the best opposition which could be mustered by the senator for Tok-ai-Do. These were men and women, all of them, who had spent half their lives engaging in wars of verbal agility and who had been selected for their talents in that sphere. Dak was a poet, a performer it is true but without experience of diplomatic argument. He feared he would be outclassed and outmanoeuvred.

He met the small crew as they came aboard in the few days before departure. They seemed a decent enough bunch, bland and not given to sabre-rattling, carrying out a duty rather than a crusade. The nervous itching between Dak's shoulder-blades gradually subsided and he stopped anticipating murderous assault around every corner.

Command of the *Leviathan* had been given to a Navy captain who, though a citizen of Tok-ai-Do as was Sitje Van Meeker, was equally not of Japanese descent. Ilya Antonovitch Stavrogin was a short, blond Slav who wore his very obvious physical difference as he wore his seniority: as something he was prepared not to emphasise just so long as everyone realised he had it. From the moment of his arrival he assumed total command of the great alien vessel, padding around the flight-deck like a smaller but equally self-assured version of Sharm, treating Dak with the courteous disregard due supercargo. At first Dak found it disconcerting to be treated as a guest in what he regarded as his home; then he was amused at how quickly he had been deposed from his position as focus of the enterprise. He smiled and kept his counsel, and hoped Captain Stavrogin and his crew would be as philosophical when and if he decided to give them the push.

The party was completed an hour before take-off with the arrival on board of the last voyager. Dak was expecting no one else. He was with the rest of the crew on the flight-deck, watching Stavrogin call the checks Divik had called and Peter Bassett watching as he had watched Divik five months ago on Ganymede, when Divik was alive and Sharm was alive and Dak was a youth with no knowledge of pain or politics or the people. As he watched he felt the slight grating vibration as the main hatch, closed after Bassett's arrival some hours earlier, opened once again, so he went down through the technical area to see what was happening.

From the top of the ramp he saw Honda at the bottom.

His stomach contracted with the memory of fear. His hands clenched into unconscious fists and in the palms the sweat started. He thought, "I don't want that man on my ship," and was startled to realise he had spoken aloud.

The rating who was carrying Honda's bag looked alarmed. "He has the necessary documentation, sir."

"I don't care. I don't want him on this ship." Dak's voice was thick and blurred. His eyes smouldered darkly.

Honda, still approaching, said reasonably, "I, too, have been ordered to Pax Mundi."

"Then take that Imperial battle-cruiser."

"I wasn't offered it. My orders attach me to Captain Stavrogin's command."

"*Leviathan* may be under Stavrogin's command, but until someone with a better claim turns up she's my ship. Do you suppose I care about your orders?"

Honda kept walking quietly up the ramp until he was within arm's reach of Dak, who had to marshal all his self-control to keep from falling back a pace. "You're still afraid of me. Well, that's all right. I gave you a bad time; you're entitled to your scars. But there's no reason for us to remain enemies. It's out of our hands now. The Senate will decide what's to be done. What happened between you and I was purely professional: I was doing my duty, you what you conceived to be yours. It's behind us now. I shouldn't dwell on it, if I were you."

"Professional?" Dak's voice shook and he didn't care. "Well, it may have seemed professional to you, but to me it felt profoundly personal. You damn near picked me apart with your drugs and your questions and your clever devices. You'd have killed me any way you had to to learn what I know. There isn't a man aboard *Leviathan* who wouldn't throw up if he saw what you do in the name of duty. You may come on board my ship. It may be I couldn't stop you if I tried. I'll tolerate your proximity because I must, but I don't want your company and I don't want your friendship. And remember this. Since all this began seventeen men have tried to destroy me. You're the only one still alive. The others died aboard this ship."

The pilot came aboard *Leviathan* while Pax Mundi was but a pinprick on the star-screen. Ostensibly his function was to guide the vessel through the teeming traffic lanes around the sovereign heart of the Alliance. In reality all the complex navigational mathematics was done by traffic control in direct communication with onboard computers, and the presence of the human pilot was to ensure that new arrivals from the space-lanes were all and only what they claimed to be: that vessels declaring themselves to be unarmed were not in fact Q-ships, ready to spring their guns at the drop of a veto. Battleships were not permitted to take up a parking orbit around Pax Mundi. The senators objected to discussing sensitive issues with the principals' gunboats circling over their heads.

Leviathan, carrying only the standard defensive armament against piracy, was allocated an orbit and neatly slotted into it. A senatorial barge, which was a shuttle with gold paint, conveyed Dak, Honda and the pilot to the surface.

It was the first time the protagonists had shared a confined space for more than a passing moment since Honda had given Dak to the Machine. Neither was unaware of the fact. Dak, feeling his eyes, found the big man watching him with half a smile and a small puzzled frown. He was wondering about the Machine and what had gone on inside its metal skull to prevent it from dealing with Hamiko as it had dealt with those who preceded him. None of them had brought his cause before the Alliance. None of them had afterwards been able to remember his cause. He would have liked to disassemble the Machine screw by screw to find out what had gone wrong, but its priesthood of technicians guarded it like a deity and would countenance no such outrage. The only other who might tell him was now under the protection of the Senate.

Across the cabin Dak was wrestling with an angel. The angel said that hatred was an illogical emotional response to fear, and Dak remembered the table. The angel said violent feelings did more damage to originator than to the object, and Dak heard again the long, silent scream from his brain when they strapped him down and wired him up. The angel said that nothing from the past could reach through to the present and hurt again unless its nightmares were shut up in the dark, nurtured lovingly and given every opportunity to consume their keeper in an ultimate black blossoming. Behind a pale, set mask which betrayed no emotion, Dak's rage expanded until it encompassed momentarily even Peter Bassett; and then it began to wane, until by the time the barge touched down on Pax Mundi he could contemplate Honda and all he represented without fear or hatred or even anger, just sorrow and a deep regret that his people and his beautiful planet could have spawned such corruption, such poverty of ideals. As they emerged through the hatch Dak looked at his old tormentor and smiled. "You've already lost."

He was only half right.

Many hours later he sat alone in a small dark ante-room, the door to the assembly hall a little ajar, its noise and colour reaching him faintly. It was all surprisingly gaudy: more like a three-ring circus than an august assembly of planetary ambassadors, he had thought as he took his place on the dais; but, then, he was used to performing in stroboscopic surroundings. Limelight didn't worry him, though the absence of audience feedback did at first.

All the senators were human, that is, descended from foundation stock on Earth. Indigenous races were not represented. When he realised, quite early, that he was not moving them Dak was tempted to slap them from their self-important apathy with the fact that it was their ancestors under discussion; but it was too dangerous. If the ploy should not work the people would be lost, their vantage known. So he ploughed on, hating them, throwing first rational argument then increasingly emotional appeal at the rows of unresponsive heads above the multi-coloured robes. They were the wisest, most powerful men in the Twelve Circles, and they dressed like peacocks. Zen help us all, Dak thought as, his repertoire of arguments exhausted, he brought the circus to a finale. I might as well have stayed on the funny farm back home.

The circus was not in fact over. When Dak yielded the floor the Ambassador of Tok-ai-Do, with Honda seated in plain view beside him, made reply. It was a well-orchestrated performance, dignified, with the accent on indignation. That such things should be said of Tok-ai-Do! That her motives should be judged anything but pure! That anyone might give credence to a half-crazed poet, who was a traitor to boot, rather than to an accredited ambassador of fifteen years' standing! Dak stayed long enough to get the gist of his address, and to appreciate his cynical professionalism, then hunted out somewhere to wait quietly for the judgement.

After the ambassador finished speaking there was a long recess. A respectful servant brought Dak refreshments on a tray but he hardly touched it. He didn't feel anxious, he didn't feel anything, just that once again he had pinned his faith on something which had failed to justify his confidence.

When the Master of the Rolls (peacock purple) took his position in front of the Senate, Dak moved to the open door to listen.

He was a thickly set man of middle years, balding under the high surcope, with a dignity Dak was sad to find indissolubly cemented with pomposity. His physical structure marked him as hailing from one of the inner circles, the oldest part of the Alliance. Descendants of those first western pioneers were afforded a special deference in the Alliance: after Earth, their civilisations were the oldest. Now they were the oldest quite. Their language was the common language of the Alliance, taught together with its mother-tongue to every human child in the Twelve Circles.

"We have heard the embassy of Dak Hamiko of Tok-ai-Do. We have heard the embassy of His Excellency the Ambassador of the Planetary Government of Tok-ai-Do. We are confused and disturbed by much that we have learned.

"Each planet within the Alliance of Known Worlds is a sovereign state governed by its traditional authorities without reference to this body, requiring neither our consent nor our approval for its administration. We would not have it otherwise. The Alliance exists to further its members' joint interests, not to homogenise their internal structures, and this Senate is a forum for mutually beneficial debate and agreement, neither a legislature nor an instrument of censure. Nevertheless, if we are to function in a cohesive and consistent fashion, it is desirable that certain values and standards be accepted by member states as constant.

"From what we have heard – though this Senate is not a court, to weigh evidence or measure guilt – it would appear that values and standards practised on Tok-ai-Do differ significantly from those promulgated in this Chamber. This is disappointing; but more disturbing is the lack of candour exhibited by the representatives of that State. It may be that Tok-ai-Do could give good and adequate reasons for continuing practices which most civilised worlds have long been able to abandon. But we have not heard them. What we have heard from the Ambassador of Tok-ai-Do, today and previously, suggests no moral or pragmatic difference between his State and others in the Alliance. Until a short time ago we had no knowledge of the means used by officers of that State to ensure civil obedience. We may feel angry that such things happen; or, if they be necessary, that they have been kept from us by what can only be a deliberate policy.

"But this Senate is not a court, has no jurisdiction in the internal affairs of Tok-ai-Do, and is not met to hear complaints against its member. We are met to decide the future of a small group of sentient beings in suspended animation on a planet whose location we do not know. For the deplorable secrecy which has characterised this entire affair extends also to Dak Hamiko, who has refused to give full information about the people in the care of the machine he refers to as the Matrix. We may understand his reasons for this, we may sympathise, certainly we may respect his courage in safeguarding his secret, but our job is not made easier by both parties to the dispute telling the Senate only what they wish it to know.

"Dak Hamiko tells us that the sleepers were an insurance policy taken out by their parents against a holocaustal disaster which ultimately overtook their planet, and should be allowed to fulfil their destiny unhampered. Tok-ai-Do argues that supervision is not only desirable, because they will be a new race in need of adult guidance, but necessary for the safety of the Alliance, because they carry the seeds of a culture which destroyed itself by greed and violence – seeds which they may sow among us to bring the Alliance too to an eventual conflagration.

"We have considered these arguments. We find that truth may lie in one quarter while wisdom lies in another. We believe that what Dak Hamiko desires is best for the sleepers, while what Tok-ai-Do requests – power of mandate – is best for the Alliance.

"But our own feelings, even though they represent the corporate will of the Alliance, do not blind us to a fundamental question which we cannot answer. Has the Senate, or the Alliance itself, any jurisdiction over the people and their planet? We do not know where it is. If it is outside the Twelve Circles, as seems likely, on purely geographic grounds our influence cannot be more than minimal. If the people are not humanoid, we cannot claim even remote kinship to them and any approach must be made as friends or as conquerors. Moreover, unless we alter the rules of this Assembly, no indigenous race, however advanced, has a right of admission."

Oh, brother, thought Dak, if you only knew!

"Our decision, then, is dependent upon factors which we cannot resolve. Our ruling is this. If the people are awake and masters of their environment when the envoys of Tok-ai-Do – or any other planetary state – arrive they must be considered a sovereign nation. But if the first arrivals from the Twelve Circles find a planet without sapient inhabitants – and for these purposes that must mean a people awake and functioning – that planet may fairly be considered a territorial acquisition and the sleepers, if they can be roused, a colonial race of the parent state. If that is the case, and particularly if they are the true descendants of the advanced civilisation Dak Hamiko has described, we are unanimous in our view that they should be afforded the rights and dignities which this Senate expects to be ubiquitous throughout the Alliance."

And that, thought Dak as he stole away from the pomp and glitter of the Chamber, is as neat a piece of fence-sitting as you'll see anywhere.

He was, of course, disappointed; but he had not come this far without a contingency plan. What was required of him now was courage and timing. His courage was battered and his timing deplorable, but his need to succeed was great and it drove him with the strength of desperation.

The Senate entertained its supplicants to supper. Having failed to satisfy either party to any marked degree, Their Excellencies seemed to feel that the least they could do was give them a good feed before sending them back into space. A shuttle brought the men down from *Leviathan*, the Ambassador of Tok-ai-Do – his knuckle-rapping not withstanding – attended, beaming, surrounded by wife and devastatingly well-drilled children, while the great hall flocked and twittered with the tropic birds who represented a thousand disparate worlds each in their own lands' fineries. Here were white-skinned blond-haired Scands, severely tailored in haunting grey and lilac; there were ebony Africs in flowing robes of cactus-flower hue; there passed an olive-patinated Asian, his puritan white at once relieved and mocked by details of fine gold thread. A Senate shindig was nothing if not extravagant.

Honda, eating methodically from a dainty platter grasped in his giant hand as he wandered the hall, wondered about the differences between people. He wondered that one small, antique planet could have produced such a varied humanity in the comparatively short time of man's sojourn there, and also that in the millennia since the Diaspora the limitless tracts and opportunities of space should have produced no further permutations; as if Earth were the natural cradle of mankind, the only laboratory where the human experiment could succeed, so that if men should dwell among the stars for aeons still all their development should be in their Earthbound past.

But this train of thought caused him less discomfort than the other which rattled his points, which was concerned with what Dak Hamiko intended next. He had come to Pax Mundi seeking the intervention and protection of the Senate, and he had failed to secure them. But Honda knew him too intimately to suppose he would now abandon his mission. However impractical, he would try to fulfil his task as long as he remained free to do so. He might abandon *Leviathan* and acquire the services of another vessel; yet he could not be unaware that, given the ruling of the Senate, anywhere he went a ship of Tok-ai-Do would be at his shoulder, ready to take control when he should lead the way to the sleepers. What would he do? Quatro-dimensional navigation made it all but impossible for one vessel to shake free of another leaving the same place at the same time. Tok-ai-Do could shadow him through all the infinite universe, and he could not go to rouse the sleepers without leading Honda or his successors straight there, should it be six months from now or ten years. If Tok-ai-Do had one virtue, it was patience.

He hoped to get some insight into the troublesome poet's mind this evening on Pax Mundi. Earlier Hamiko had announced his intention of acquainting the assembly with his plans. Everyone present was eager to hear him, not least the crew of *Leviathan*, but Hamiko made no move towards the rostrum: each time Honda checked, moving casually around the throng strangling his plate, Dak was in the same corner, deep in conversation with Peter Bassett, oblivious of the expectant hall behind him.

If he were determined to beat Tok-ai-Do to the sleepers – and nothing in their acquaintance disposed Honda to think that his devotion to them might at this point falter – then he might make a last attempt to persuade his companions or seduce their consciences to his ends, but after that had failed sooner or later he would resort, since violence would achieve nothing and was anyway outside his ethics, to trickery. He did not require a prodigious head start, just enough of a margin for him to suborn transport and get away into star-drive with nobody close enough to plot or pursue him. Honda had taken the precaution of scattering loyalty money among the private operators on Pax Mundi and was reasonably confident that Hamiko would be unable to hire a deep-space vessel without it coming swiftly to his notice; while stealing a vessel from a major spaceport would be a doomed enterprise for the most accomplished felon, which Dak Hamiko was not.

Still Honda's eye kept travelling across the brilliant crowd to the slender figure in the corner, distinct in gentle black. Because if he intended treachery there would be much in favour of an early gambit. All he needed was a short time free from scrutiny, and a sympathetic or greedy or just plain stupid pilot, and he could be safe in the trackless maze of superspace, immune to detection until he should emerge on the far side at his destination. Wherever that was.

The thought began as a bad joke, a kind of wry satire on himself, but he found to his increasing discomfort that he could not dismiss it as such. It was exactly the sort of move a thinker like Hamiko might make: lull them all into a sense of false security with his announcement and, while they were patiently waiting, disappear. Yet there the man was, plain for all the assembly to see, exactly where he had been all evening.

At least, thought the policeman, his unease quickening, there was somebody tall and thin with dark hair and black clothes. Earlier it was certainly Hamiko rabbiting away earnestly to Dr Bassett; but it was getting to be a long time since Honda had seen his face. Recognising the notion as neurotic if not paranoid, yet also knowing he would have no rest now until he laid it, Honda vented a resigned sigh and put down his plate and glass. Conscious of the eyes of the gathering upon him – for most of those present knew something of what had passed between him and the poet and were interested in any confrontation which might ensue – and hoping he could do this without provoking a diplomatic incident, he walked across the room and laid a hand on Hamiko's bony shoulder.

Peter Bassett observed, "Most women object to being manhandled by perverts they haven't been introduced to," and Honda, stunned, found himself in receipt of an icy glare from a tall, slender, dark-haired girl he had never seen, wearing Dak Hamiko's travel-worn clothes.

Dr Bassett was grinning.

Ilya Stavrogin was not smiling ten minutes later when he strode into the traffic control office at the spaceport, Honda and the Tok-ai-Do ambassador at his heels. "I left my vessel in a parking orbit around your planet in the belief that it would remain there until I returned," he snapped, beginning without preamble as he came through the door. "I now find that while I was enjoying the hospitality of the Senate you permitted it to be pirated. One somehow expects a little more care to be taken at the hub of the Alliance."

The controller was unflustered and impenitent. "Piracy is the appropriation of a vessel by those who have no right to it. *Leviathan* was checked out by her registered owner. No crime has occurred."

"When did he go?"

"Perhaps an hour ago."

"Alone?"

"So far as I know."

"Where was he heading?"

"Into superspace. He filed no flight plan."

"And you did not plot his trajectory."

"I had no reason to. There was nothing abnormal about his departure."

"In spite of the fact that he left his crew behind at a Senatorial beanfeast?"

"It is no business of traffic control if an owner should choose to dismiss his crew. If he has broken a contract with you, that is a matter for civil complaint. I was satisfied that the computer aboard *Leviathan* was capable of navigating the vessel safely and thus had no reason to detain him. And now, if you'll excuse me, the lanes become increasingly busy at this time of day –"

Stavrogin leaned across the man's desk, his knuckles white on the white plastic. "Beaching a crew may not be a crime. But both murder and kidnapping are, and one or the other has happened aboard *Leviathan* because I left a crewman on board when I came down to the surface and there is no way he would voluntarily set off for a week's jolly among the stars in the company of a mad poet who doesn't know Aldebaran from Antares."

Chapter Eight

The last thing in Dak's mind as the service shuttle locked on to *Leviathan's* hatch was that there might be someone on board. He knew the Senate's invitation had extended to the ship's complement, and he had seen Honda and Stavrogin and others of the crew in the hall before sneaking away to exchange clothes with the mischievous elder daughter of a Tok-ai-Do commissioner. (Fortunately, it was her idea of fashion, or perhaps her way of thumbing her nose at the older generation, to turn up for a Senate function in work-shirt and dungarees.)

He dismissed the shuttle with a more than cursory farewell to the pilot, thinking, That might be the last human being I see until the first of the sleepers wakes. Vague and somehow aimless, in spite of the urgent need to leave, he padded through to the flight-deck and stood a moment looking round him. Then the rim of Pax Mundi passing slowly across his screen as the ship turned in her sleep brought him back to the pressing present. Languor dispelled, he threw himself into the command seat and thumbed the console, calling up the navigational computer.

Behind him a voice said, "Touch one more button and I'll blow your arm off."

Dak could not have been more shocked had the keyboard been electrified. His hand jerked back as though burned and he started to turn, but a shower of sparks burst off the steel cabinet by his knee. He felt the brief heat of the laser and froze.

"I mean it. I'd kill you if I had to but I don't have to. All I have to do is disable you and wait for the others to return. You can still lead us to the sleepers with one arm, or with your kneecap in shards. Keep quite still until I tell you to move."

But by now Dak had got a purchase on who it was behind him and his rocketing heartbeat had begun to level off. The voice, high-pitched, classically accented and now coming very fast, belonged to Stavrogin's second lieutenant, a young navigator of the good family Ito, generations of admirals behind him and early command ahead. Dak knew little about the Navy, but he doubted if the young man was ready for responsibility.

Very aware of the weapon, and the logic of its owner's reasoning, Dak slowly spread his hand in a gesture he hoped looked friendly. "There's no need to get excited. I'm really quite harmless."

"Keep your explanations for Captain Stavrogin. And keep still!" The voice soared, momentarily out of control, and the myriad tiny nerves in Dak's skin twitched in anticipation of assault. He would have given almost anything to be able to see the lieutenant's face.

Courage and timing: Dak Hamiko set about giving the best performance of his life to his smallest ever audience. His breathing grew hard and stern, his fingers drummed once on the console and then he crossed his arms and sat back, his whole frame radiating impatience. "Right. And then I dare say he'll want to hear yours. Zen, I thought this nonsense was over. I've just spent five hours in conference with Honda, the ambassador and the Secretariat. We finally agree a compromise, I come up here to notify the Matrix and I'm set upon like a trespasser on my own ship. Didn't you understand Stavrogin's instructions, or what?" Arms still aggressively crossed, he kicked his chair round and glared at the boy, demanding an answer.

Young Ito found himself inexplicably on the defensive. "The last instructions I had from Captain Stavrogin were before he went ashore. He said –"

"Don't play the innocent with me, lad, I was with him when he called you not half an hour ago. I assume you know what the words Full Co-operation mean?"

"I received no call." Ito still held the gun, but his attention was totally diverted from it. "I've been on this bridge all evening and no call came through."

"Well, I'm not going to argue with you. Stavrogin's on his way up: he can show you how to use a communicator." Dak glanced back at the panel and his tone turned sarcastic. "Beginning with, Never lean your elbow on the cut-out button."

"I never did!" Three swift paces brought Ito to the console. All was as it should have been, but before he could make that assessment and draw a conclusion from it Dak Hamiko was moving, fast, and something was flashing in his hands.

Forgive me, thought Dak, his conscience in agony, as the crystal Sandaar – the last one, the one from the tube, no more mining for *Leviathan* – crashed against the side of the lieutenant's head and he fell on the deck as though dead. And Dak dropped the shattered crystal and knelt beside him and wanted to cry, not even so much for the boy as for his own lost innocence.

Ito awoke to a headache, an empty holster and a blank sky. *Leviathan* had already made the jump into star-drive. She would remain in superspace until palpably close to her destination, beyond reach of all radar, radio and visual communication or detection. For the period of her journey she ceased to exist except, subjectively, for those on board. She was, in the most absolute of ways, beyond pursuit.

Dak Hamiko was at the console, his back to the computer, nursing an opaque crystal rod in his arms like a statue of Kuan Yin. He smiled wanly. "When I came aboard at Ganymede we had two of these. Divik broke the first across my head."

"Ganymede? Is that where we're going?"

"No." Dak looked away, then back. "How do you feel?"

"I'm all right. Listen. Stavrogin will find us. Honda's going to get you."

"Not before –" He started again. "Not in time to stop me."

"You're going to wake them up?" Dak nodded. "I'll stop you. If there's any way at all I'll stop you."

"Why should it matter to you?"

"I am of Tok-ai-Do. I am in the service of my world. You're trying to hurt my world. I'll stop you any way I can."

"I'm not trying to hurt Tok-ai-Do. I didn't want to hurt you. I never wanted to hurt anyone. Somehow I've been backed into a corner where, whatever I do, or if I do nothing, somebody's going to suffer, at least in their own eyes. All I can do is what I think is right."

"What did they pay you? To sell out?"

For a moment Dak felt angry; then the anger dissolved and left him only tired, enervated. "They didn't pay me. It cost."

"Are you going to kill me?" Ito asked later. His face was set, ready for the answer, but it was still a young face, an absurdly young face. Dak thought there was something desperately wrong with a culture which sent its children out to fight.

"No."

"I've told you I'll oppose you. You might be wiser –"

"Whatever you do, I won't harm you. I promise."

The quickest way to make an enemy is to put someone in your debt. Ito, his pride already flayed, responded bitterly. "You're a fool. What's to stop me now from taking this ship back? If our positions had been reversed, I'd have killed you at the first opportunity."

"Probably," agreed Dak. "But then, probably you'll never be entrusted with the fate of a nation." It was an arrogant remark, uncharacteristically so, and no sooner was it out than Dak wished it unsaid; but he could not withdraw it without sounding still more patronising, and anyway he didn't think it that important. So he let it pass, unaware that he had dropped a match in a sump of resentment which would smoulder for a time and then explode.

Pax Mundi, in the First Circle, was considerably closer to the Solar system than Tok-ai-Do, which was in the Sixth, and the marvellous facility of super-space, enabling manned craft to take advantage of a short-cut denied to light itself, compressed a journey of light years into a period of days; but for Dak the days stretched out like an eternity. He did not dare leave the flight-deck. Ito was a naval officer, a navigator, and he was familiar with the ship. If he saw half a chance he would attempt to stop or divert *Leviathan*, or get a message to Stavrogin, who might be expected to have acquired a listening-post if not another ship by now. Ito might succeed or the Matrix might stop him; either way Dak considered the consequences worth avoiding. So he stayed by the command console and he stayed awake.

At first he found some relief from the crowding fatigue in the meditation techniques first taught him by his mother. Later he required stimulants from the ship's dispensary to keep his head from falling off his shoulders. It was an insidious weakness, that crept up behind him unannounced, that waited until he was most comfortable, most relaxed and at ease, and then sent him sprawling across the coloured lights like a drunk. Each time the movement proved enough to rouse him from the craved oblivion. Twice he found Ito half out of his seat, subsiding as Dak shook the mists from his head. More often he was just sitting, watching, an expectant smile on his youthful, ruthless face. All that kept him from a rush attack was the certainty that the risk was unnecessary, that Dak would keel over before *Leviathan* reached her destination.

While Ito watched, smiling, Dak was going through a small private hell, made more trying by the knowledge that it was largely of his own making. There were locked doors on *Leviathan*: he could have put Ito behind any of them and slept away the remaining days in uninterrupted peace. But Ito would not submit quietly, and Dak was not prepared to use violence. As long as the lieutenant thought Dak would pass out in the end he would wait passively. All Dak had to do was stay awake.

Animals deprived of sleep become profoundly disturbed and may die. Men manage on the whole better, particularly some men who through a physiological or psychological abnormality can go most of their lives with little or no sleep. Unhappily, Dak was not among them. He ached with weariness. His chest felt constricted, his limbs cramped – he didn't know where to put himself for the best. When he stood up he felt dizzy, and when he moved his head it took seconds for his eyes to catch up. Finally, when he found himself considering the possibility of dissolving the stimulant and mainlining it for increased effect, he called a halt. Viewing Ito askance across the flight-deck, because one eye was quite wide while the other was almost battened down behind its curtain of little scars, he said

– or rather slurred – "I'm getting fed up with this."

"Sleep it off."

"I will if you will."

"It's not my bedtime."

"Seems – impolite, somehow – to sleep in company."

"Don't mind me. I've plenty to keep me occupied."

"Will you sleep if I tell you a story?"

"What?"

"A bedtime story. You know. Like your mother used to."

"What are you talking about?"

"You mean your mother never told you stories? Ito, that's your problem, that's why you don't trust people. You had a deprived childhood."

"You're cracking up. I think you've taken too many of those pills. You're going to pass out any minute."

"Perhaps. But at least my mother told me stories. At least I know about the worm."

"Worm."

"Yes, worm. You know – long, thin things, they burrow through the earth. People don't appreciate worms. All they see is a primitive animal sucking in soil at one end, spitting it out at the other and digesting anything worth having in between. But worms have personalities too. Very passionate, worms. Very sensitive. Highly developed political acumen. Moral and courageous, and they never tell lies. If a thing's worth having it's worth fighting for, worms think, and if it's worth fighting for it's worth killing for. They also believe everything they're told. Just about Tok-ai-Do's notion of the ideal citizen, are worms, 'cept they do make a mess in the garden."

"You're drunk."

"I wish I was. At least I'd have enjoyed getting like this. Also, they're devoted little home-makers – worms. Highly territorial. Consider good fences make good neighbours. Anyway, one day this worm sticks his head out of his burrow just to make sure everything's as it should be, and there, not six inches away, sticking out of an adjacent hole, is another worm. Far too close for comfort.

After all, we've no idea what kind of worm he is. He might insult our worm's wife, corrupt his children, vote Christian Democrat or crack his egg at the little end. An unknown quantity so near to home is a cause for concern; more, a case for action."

"I see now why you tell these stories at bedtime. The idea is to bore children to sleep."

"Our worm draws himself up and quivers violently; from a worm this is very threatening behaviour. The other worm responds in like fashion. Our worm takes several deep breaths to make himself look bigger. The other worm also swells. Our worm emits a noxious odour guaranteed to clear the lawn for three paces in any direction. The smell from the other worm nearly knocks him back down his hole.

"There's nothing else for it but war and the victory of the stronger worm over the weaker. Our worm, with a cry of 'Dulce et decorum est pro patria mori' – which is Latin for 'It is sweet and fitting to die for the wormland' – makes a headlong dash across the turf and grabs his protagonist by the throat. But the stronger-worm fights back: pain shoots through our worm's body as alien fangs sink into his flesh. The harder he fights, the worse the pain, but he keeps on fighting until, finally, he drops dead. So, simultaneously, does the other worm. The blackbird who enjoys the remains with his elevenses knows the answer."

"What answer?" demanded Ito, torn between impatience and a crazy fascination.

"There was only one worm. It had two ends."

Ito stared at him. "That's it? That's the punchline? Is it supposed to have some significance? Does it mean something?"

"We're heading for Earth. The people – the sleepers – they're the last Earthmen."

There was a long, crawling silence. Then, "They *can't* be," shrilled Ito, outraged, "it's a lie."

"All right," said Dak. "I'm going to sleep now."

"No, *wait* a minute. Admit you lied." The young navigator came to his feet and advanced, his slim body hunched menacingly, like a stick-insect doing an impression of a Sumo wrestler. "I'll make you admit it."

"I've already admitted it. We're not heading for Earth, there are no Earthmen, there can't be, it's a lie; goodnight."

"Stay awake, damn you! What kind of a trick are you playing now?"

"I'm not. It's just that I've had this. I've been beaten, starved, shot, drugged and deprived of sleep. I've been violated, physically and psychologically, by men and machines. I've been frightened for most of the last six months; for substantial parts of that time I've been mortally terrified. I've been told that this was my duty or that was my duty, and that my allegiance was due to these people or to those people. Well, I've done the best I could for as long as I could, but now I'm too tired to do any more. It's your problem now. Take *Leviathan* out of star-drive if you want to, radio Stavrogin where we are. Tell him they're his ancestors, and yours, and mine. Tell him to shoot them out of the sky if that's what his orders demand. The prospect shouldn't bother him unduly: he isn't Japanese."

Ito was staring at him with a kind of impotent fury. "You bastard!" he choked when his overwrought emotions found tongue. "You half-breed bastard!"

Dak hadn't been called that since he was a child. It had hurt very much then. Nothing hurt now. "Yes, I'm only half Japanese, with presumably only half our traditional onus of respect for our forebears. But look what I've done. I've gone through everything but death itself to save the ancestors from slavery. I'd have succeeded, too, if it hadn't been for you. But, as you say, I'm only a half-breed bastard. If you're sure about my innate inferiority, you must also believe that someone of better caste could have done more. If I'd been of the noble family Ito, my unblemished pedigree a direct link between me and those people on Earth, perhaps I could have done more. Perhaps I could have finished it. Just think: one of them may be an Ito too."

With that, and a small, enigmatic shrug, Dak rose from the console – not without difficulty, for his body felt desperately heavy – and walked off the flight-deck and to his cabin. Ito stood alone in the command centre and stared at the console with its instruments that he knew so well – these that would bring *Leviathan* out of superspace, those which would broadcast her whereabouts to the Twelve Circles – and could not touch them. Rage surged under his tunic, because he knew he was being manipulated, but the taboo, springing from race memory deeper than any training, forbade him any action, or even thought, against the ancestors. He was a victim not of Hamiko's persuasion but of his own rigid culture, which in reality allowed no more individual discretion now on Tok-ai-Do than millennia ago in Japan under the Shogun before the black ships brought the Western notion of freedom.

So Ito stayed by the console, staring at its controls and doing nothing, while conflicting compulsions tore him apart; and when Dak awoke fourteen hours later it was to the voice of the Matrix, welcoming him back as computers guided *Leviathan* into orbit around the Earth.

Neither Honda nor Stavrogin slept, at least not for more than minutes at a time. Stavrogin had too much to do, and Honda had too much to think about.

Within a couple of hours of stamping out of the traffic office Stavrogin had acquired a ship. It was a yacht, small and fast, and it belonged to the senator from Iskra, a Russian settled planet with close cultural ties to Stavrogin's own. Out among the stars, what you were and what you were doing counted for less than who your ancestors were. Racism took on galactic dimensions. The irony of it would have left Dak breathless, but there was at that time no one else in the Twelve Circles capable of appreciating it.

While Stavrogin was shaking his family-tree and waiting for a senatorial yacht to drop out, Honda was thinking about Dak Hamiko; specifically, where with the entire universe at his disposal he would go. To the sleepers, patently, and no one else knew where they were. Then where had he come from when he arrived back at Tok-ai-Do?

Communications in deep space were hardly faster than star-drive vessels; Honda could not immediately wire off an APB of the Have

You Seen This Ship? variety because most of the Alliance would not receive it for weeks and any reply would take twice as long. All he had to go on were two pieces of information which had been available to him most of the time he had Hamiko: that *Leviathan* was a helium miner until her crew went missing, and that her last known port of call before Tok-ai-Do was a dusty little staging-post called Ganymede, in a dwindling solar system in a remote spiral arm of the old Milky Way, where the Alliance began.

Life would have been easier for Honda if a record of Dak's deportation by the Ganymede security forces had survived; but the Matrix, which had doctored the accounts to produce that result, doctored them again to erase all record of it. The officers involved remembered, of course, but when a culture is based on the retrieval circuits of high-priced hardware, nobody asks people.

Honda consulted the star charts. Sol was a suitable star for mining helium, and Ganymede was the last spaceport. But *Leviathan* had not reached Sol. The black box recorder had been wiped but there was no evidence of recent mining activity: no helium in the holds, no fresh scorching, and a heat-shield newly fitted on Ganymede was unbaptised. Honda did not know where the chain of events culminated, but he thought it began not too far from Ganymede.

Stavrogin set the space yacht speeding for Jupiter.

Dak, almost as groggy from sleep as he had been from lack of it, staggered onto the flight-deck, the familiar voice resounding in his ears. He found Ito rooted to the spot and dislodged him with a friendly slap. "There's no need to be afraid."

"At last," grumbled the Matrix. "You have kept me waiting again, Dak Hamiko."

"I apologise," Dak smiled, impenitent. "It was not entirely my fault."

The machine's tone softened. "How are you now?"

"I'm all right. Everything's all right. Everything's going to be all right. Do you know the terms of the Senate's decision?"

"Of course."

"Of course. Then you know we've all but succeeded. Is there any sign of pursuit?"

The Matrix was uncharacteristically cagey. "I cannot be sure. Nothing shows on my screens."

"If I didn't know you better," Dak said slyly, "I'd think you were momentarily doubting your own powers. You are, after all, the Matrix –"

"As you know perfectly well," the Matrix interrupted coolly, "vessels in superspace generate no signal which can be received in real space. There is nothing in real space closer than Ganymede, and nothing in the Solar System coming this way. Tok-ai-Do is too distant for any expedition to get here in time to do anything useful, and there are no armed divisions on Pax Mundi except the Senatorial Guard. And yet –"

"Yet?"

"I feel – uneasy."

"Leave the suspense neuroses to we humans who wouldn't know a logic circuit if it smacked us in the eye. Come and get me: I'll set your mind at rest."

"The lander is closing with you now."

"I want to go down too," said Ito. It was the first time he had spoken, reminding the Matrix that Dak was not alone.

"Who is your companion?"

Dak frowned, thinking. While he thought he said, "His name is Ito. He is a compatriot of mine – from Tok-ai-Do. Ito, this is the Matrix." What he was wondering was, if he and Ito made planetfall together, whether Tok-ai-Do could then be said to have reached the people in time to claim some say in their destiny. If a loophole existed, men like Honda could be relied upon to find it. "No," he said finally. "Be patient. Follow me down when I've done what I came back for. I'll show you round then."

"You don't trust me," sneered the young man.

"I will ensure that he causes no trouble," promised the Matrix in a low voice.

Dak's head came up sharply. "This man is my friend and under my protection. You will not threaten him. Under no circumstances will you lay so much as a microwatt upon him."

"Lemmings take greater care of themselves than you do," growled the Matrix. "Come now, or Sol will be a white dwarf before we settle the fate of my poor, patient people." They left Ito alone on the bridge of the *Leviathan*, all but shut down in her holding orbit, smouldering.

Chapter Nine

The space yacht *Edge of Eternity* warped out of superspace in the area between Ganymede and the asteroid belt, and simultaneously sent a locator signal flashing across every available band. Ito aboard *Leviathan* received it in the same moment that the Matrix did, but Ito, who had used it himself in other circumstances, knew exactly what it was while the Matrix could only surmise and, while the Matrix was still evaluating, Ito responded.

"Confound that treacherous animal!" cried the Matrix, with such a passion of hatred that Dak froze in his tracks halfway down the communicator shaft from the lander silo, his skin crawling.

"What's happened?"

The Matrix explained tersely, its mechanical voice somehow thick with fury. "I should have killed him when you arrived. You should have killed him before you came, you squeamish coward!"

"If I cared less about life," Dak shot back, trying to beat down his anger at this monstrous injustice, "I should not have endured everything I have to protect those of the sleepers. I will not have Ito harmed; or any of them. How long before they get here?"

"Minutes."

"Then we'd better get on with it." And picking up his weary body with muscles that had lost their spring and tendons their resilience, he ran down the shaft.

Ito, spinning slowly in the shapeless silence above Earth's roiling atmosphere, was without equilibrium. His existence, hitherto uncomplicated, had lost direction, dimension. He was confused, ashamed and bitterly angry. Against all his training and experience,

Dak Hamiko had made him question the duty of his allegiance. When Hamiko was there, filling the flight-deck with his calm voice and serene presence, what he said sounded reasonable and right, even to a man like Ito in whom instinct, upbringing, teaching and self-interest all combined to urge him to loyalty and obedience. Nothing – not bribery, blackmail or torture – could have deflected him from that preprogrammed course, save only the simplistic appeal of the magnetic, messianic persona with whom fate had decreed he must share the infinity of superspace. The loneliness made men vulnerable, so that anyone could be misled by strange pleadings.

But when the familiar, commanding voice of Ilya Stavrogin reached into the ticking silence, clear and unaffected as if from the next room – which, relatively speaking, it was – the spell which Hamiko had woven dissolved, duty and obligation came flooding back, and Ito, to his credit, responded to the call without pausing to formulate a plausible explanation for his dereliction.

Only when he signed off and sat back to await his commander's arrival did he fall to contemplating all his shattered hopes, and to seeking excuses for his negligence in first losing control of *Leviathan* and then failing to wrest it back, at the first or any of several subsequent opportunities, from a solitary pacifist poet. The jar that was *Edge of Eternity* locking against the universal hatch brought him shooting from his seat with renewed military fervour and a determination to restore the polish to his tarnished reputation.

"They're coming in for a landing," reported the Matrix. It had been giving a running commentary since the little craft first appeared in the Solar System. For most of the same time Dak had been running. Now he leaned against the white plastic wall, gasping for breath, sure that his lungs must burst. It seemed incredible that a ship, even with star-drive, could get here from Ganymede in less time than it took a man to run from the lander silo to the hollow heart of the Matrix. "Someone up there must fancy his skills as a pilot."

"Stavrogin," grunted Dak. "Never mind him. What do I do

now?"

"The manual override is located at the top of the calandria. It is normally approached by a service shute above this one. But I intend to batten down the hatches in the upper levels to (*a*) keep them out, and (*b*) slow them down if they do get in. I can hold them long enough for you to do the job, if you've a head for heights."

"Heights?"

"You'll have to enter the calandria at this level and climb up the inside of the shaft to the override position. It is not particularly far up, and there are access ladders; but it's a very long way down."

Dak squeezed beads of perspiration out of his eyes. "Have I any choice?"

"Not really."

"Then show me where to go."

As he squirmed through the narrow service hatch and saw the vast open cylinder of the calandria yawn away beneath him, its curved plastic face like a jetbike rider's Wall of Death but hung with cables and conduits and a dizzy network of ladders as fine and tenuous as cobweb, the Matrix said, "They are down safely."

"I wish I was," muttered Dak, swinging into space.

The airlock doors of the surface complex defied the landing-party scant moments. They had been built to withstand the elements, the remote possibility of predators and the remoter one of primitive weapons. The men who built them could have had no concept of the systems available to soldiers of Stavrogin's generation. The absence of power to the upper levels certainly hindered progress through the dark bulwarked corridors; but Honda was a powerful man. With Stavrogin blasting the mechanisms and Honda shouldering aside the hatches they managed well enough. Ito carried the light. Others who had come on *Edge of Eternity* stayed with the vessel. If the pursuers could catch up with Hamiko, three were more than enough to stop him; if they couldn't, extra personnel were no help and pointlessly at risk, and a swift departure might be indicated.

Since collecting him from *Leviathan*, Stavrogin had hardly spoken to Ito. There had been time for nothing but the tersest exchange of information on Hamiko's whereabouts and intentions, certainly none for a philosophic discussion on why a naval officer in a position to do his clear duty should fall short of doing it. But from the moment he found the lieutenant alive and well and alone on *Leviathan*'s flight-deck, Stavrogin had treated him with undisguised contempt. Even Honda, who had been more deeply involved in the affair for longer, was not ready to condemn the young man unheard, but Stavrogin was not interested in his excuses. Partly it was the tension of the moment, partly the prospect of a narrow defeat which might in other circumstances have been a victory; partly it was that particular scorn which brave, unimaginative men reserve for anything that smacks of compromise. For all these reasons, and perhaps others, the captain reacted to Ito as a man might to a bug, or a noxious smell. Ito bit his lip and carried the torch and saluted with the utmost punctiliousness, while his heart cried for vengeance.

Tok-ai-Do was a gentle, rolling world, and the national taste in trees ran to bonsai. Dak climbed the spun-steel web a little like a sloth and a little like an orang: rather slowly and very, very carefully. Below him the plummeting cylinder diminished to a pinprick. Ranged round those remotely deep levels were the cryogenic chambers and the gene banks: the seminal reason for the Matrix. When he had been down there Dak had not appreciated how deep in the protective earth it was. Higher were the living quarters, a self-contained township which had had one resident in the last five millennia, and he a transient. Up where Dak was going were only machines: the nuclear pile, generators, air filters, water purifiers, the maintenance department, and the manual override.

Looking up made him dizzy, looking down made him sick. He fixed his eyes on a point three rungs above his head and kept them there, climbing doggedly, shifting one hold at a time, gripping the thin rungs so hard that the muscles along his forearms clenched and spasmed and those behind his shoulders knotted into a painful slab. His thighs ached and quivered, and sweat ran down his face in rivers and down his body inside his clothes. He could not have said whether the breathlessness which racked his chest was due to exertion or fear. He could not have said anything.

When the ladder intersected with a catwalk he took it, because the override position was across the shaft from where he started. Changing from vertical to horizontal locomotion and then back again seemed the most hazardous part of an altogether perilous exploit.

Stavrogin, who had been leading the incursion at a run, weapon in hand, paused to allow the lumbering, powerful Honda to catch up. Eyeing Ito oddly, he stood aside to let him pass. "On second thoughts," he said, "you had better go first."

Ito brightened and shouldered through smartly. It was about the first remark the captain had addressed directly to him since leaving *Leviathan*: it had to be better than that chilling disregard. Also, it gave him a chance to vindicate himself. If he died in their defence, Stavrogin would not speak his name with scorn, and his family would be spared the ignominy of a court martial; so Ito reasoned.

"Don't look so damned noble," sneered the Russian. "It's just that, with your form, I'd rather have you in front of me than behind me."

Honda, panting, looked at them both – two small men as full of anger as fighting cocks – and wished he had the breath left to knock their heads together.

The last hatch was almost the death of Honda. The power came back on as he braced his shoulder against it and, its locking mechanism blasted away, it slid swiftly back, all but pitching him over the sill. And over the sill was nothing but a pristine functional glare and a straight drop towards the centre of the earth. The hatch gave on to the calandria, and there was no platform on the inside, only the catwalk and the ladders.

And Dak Hamiko, on the far side of the calandria, thirty metres away across the yawning pit and half that distance above their heads, at the end of the catwalk, where it stopped at a small control point. There appeared to be just one instrument.

He was leaning against the wall, hands on knees, bent almost double over his heaving chest when the hatch slid back. He saw the three men as they saw him, saw Stavrogin's weapon swinging up, knew the Matrix would react and tried to forestall it. Pushing one hand out in front of him he cried, "You're too late. The circuit has already been completed. The people are waking even now."

Stavrogin hesitated, looked at Honda. Honda nodded slowly. "I do believe he's beaten us." Louder he said, "Can the process be stopped?"

"No." The voice of the Matrix was like a granite wall. None of the three men was prepared for it; all were visibly shaken.

"You must abide by the Senate's decision," shouted Dak.

Honda, recovering first, looked at him curiously – a spiky figure suspended spiderlike above the abyss, frail-looking, vulnerable. Not a brave man by any conventional yardstick: he was afraid now, Honda seemed to see his trembling even at this distance; perhaps because he had felt him shake in the past. Nor a clever one: he had made blunders a half-witted child could have avoided. Yet he had succeeded; by enduring long enough and trying hard enough he had defeated a nation planet whose power and utter ruthlessness few people knew better than Honda who was part of them. At last he signalled consent. "That was agreed."

"It's over, then?" Try as he would, Dak could not keep the disbelief from his voice.

Honda smiled. "Over."

Over. Dak straightened up, stiffly. The urgency was over. The pain and the fear were over. The sensation of being torn in two by forces at once uncaring and unforgiving was over. He was a free man for the first time in nine months. A symbolic period. In the time it takes a woman to bring forth a child, Dak Hamiko had brought forth a nation; with the Matrix acting as midwife. He said, "There's an observation deck below. If you'd like to, come with me and watch the sleepers wake." He moved towards the ladder.

Afterwards the shocked onlookers could not agree exactly what happened. Stavrogin thought Ito just yelled. Honda thought he cried his own name. In any event the torch – still burning, despite the surfeit of light all round – went rolling across the deck and Ito's weapon flared in his hands.

Whatever the setting, at that range the blast had insufficient time to do more than stun before Stavrogin, with battle-honed reactions, knocked it aside with the first element of a blow whose culmination felled Ito unconscious on the plastic floor.

But the blast caught Dak full in the back in that peculiarly vulnerable moment as he reached for the ladder, neither still on the catwalk nor established on the rungs. The blow, like a hurled brick, broke grip and balance both; so he fell. By the time Stavrogin looked round again he was gone.

The Matrix, a cry of grief wrung from its silicon soul, made a desperate effort to counter the gravity in the calandria, but it was too little too late and served only to send the two men staring horrified in the hatchway reeling for support. With momentum gained in the first moments, the tumbling form of Dak Hamiko hit the bottom of the calandria at a speed very little short of 186 miles an hour.

For a long, utterly still moment nothing broke the terrible silence. Then a slow rumbling began in the bowels of the Matrix, a growing thunder, a deepening roar that shook the fabric of the complex with all the elemental rage of an earthquake.

"I think," Stavrogin said, "we would be better out of here." Honda bent to lift the senseless lieutenant; Stavrogin cried impatiently, "Leave him!" Then, in almost the same breath, "Sorry. Can I help?"

"Nothing and no one can help us now," muttered Honda, "if that thing decides it wants revenge."

My fault, keened the Matrix, alone in its secret synapses; my fault. They killed you but it was I who made you a target, I who failed to protect you; all through, my fault. I hurt you, they hurt you, all you ever wanted was to do what was best, now between us we've killed you. This pain is more than I can bear. I am a computer, infinitely superior to and inexpressibly different from mortal men; yet I was designed to take my place in the development of a human race, and for that I needed a maternal instinct. If it is not absurd to imagine a machine as the mother of a man, then Dak Hamiko, as a son I loved you.

The roar became a voice, deep and turbulent, filled with an atavistic hatred and unknowable grief. Made great and eternal and sentient by men long gone, the Matrix had five lost millennia to express in its mourning. "Get out. GET OUT! *GET OUT!*"

The men, Honda carrying Ito, Stavrogin covering them from behind with his ludicrously paltry weapon, fled back along the corridors the way they had come.

Dak was a free consciousness lingering in the void above his broken body. He knew what had happened without the evidence of the shattered thing, remembered it all: the blow, the wild brief struggle to regain his grip, the breathless, helpless flight of failure, right down to the microsecond of agony at the bottom of the shaft. He also knew, in the approximate, instinctive manner of a homing pigeon, what came next. He welcomed the fact that he was still capable of rational thought as a fair omen.

His mind, exploring its new parameters, brushed against the grief of the Matrix and immediately expanded to encompass it, comforting.

I never knew you felt that way about me.

Of course you didn't. You don't expect sentiment from a machine. It's my one weakness.

Laughter bubbled up through Dak's mind. I thought that was your modesty.

I shall miss you, Dak Hamiko.

You won't be alone now. You have your work to do.

I shall fulfil my function. Because of you this planet will live again. In time all men shall know what you did.

Far below new sounds merged with the perpetual mechanical hum as circuits long dormant began the processes which would rouse the sleepers. Soon those sounds would be joined by human voices.

Don't teach them to hate. Whatever I did, I did because it was due to them: owed on behalf of those who got away to those who didn't. In other circumstances they would have been our last chance. Perhaps they still are.

Stay. Watch them grow. I am a perfect force-field: within me you can live for ever.

Mentally, Dak shook his head. I, too, have a destiny to fulfil.

Before leaving he cast a last look at the twisted thing below, discarded wrapping of his transcended mortality. It had served him well enough in life. It had given him pleasure, some pain; mostly, it had taken him where he wanted to go. They had been one, closer than lovers, but its time was past, its usefulness gone; Dak felt no remaining kinship for it, more than a butterfly for its sloughed chrysalis.

I should tidy that away, if I were you. Before it upsets the children.

The heart of the Matrix swelled with the thought. There shall I have built a monument.

Dak smiled. Between you and I there is no need of such.

No. But they – They shall have need of gods.

All the gods they'll ever need are out there. The Earth, the stars – when the time is right, their brothers. If you want to tell them about me, tell them the truth – that a man, neither better nor worse than other men, believing in the future, wanted to share the universe with them but found, to his regret, that he couldn't share it, only bequeath it. Tell them it's theirs, with my blessing: to have and to hold, to love and to cherish, in its poverty and its wealth, unto all succeeding time – for death shall not part them from it, only bind them the closer to it. Theirs is the kingdom, the power and the glory, world without end. And to them – Tell them that I loved them.

The reality of the calandria was slipping, its white gleam and the massive, sorrowing mentality that was the Matrix dimming. Goodbye ... he called, and the Matrix cried his name in anguish and loss, once, and then was gone ...

A living darkness crowded in, an energetic coldness that he found both heavy and stimulating, both alien and familiar. He found that he had a body again, but it was by no means the one he was used to.

WELCOME, WANDERER, said the whale.